The Chair She Sat In

Tales from the Angels' Share
Volume 3

Marella Sands

Word Posse

Dedication

To all the writers who got me excited about ghost stories.

The Angels' Share Books

Volume 1: Through a Keyhole, Darkly
Volume 2: What the Thunder Said
Volume 3: The Chair She Sat In

Other Word Posse Books by Marella Sands

Pandora's Mirror
Fortune's Daughter
Restless Bones

Ring of Fire Press Books by Marella Sands

Perdition
Purgatory
Perfection (coming in 2020)

Visit us at www.wordposse.com

This book has been typeset in Fanwood. Cover design by Word Posse.

Copyright © 2020 by Marella Sands. All rights reserved. This book, or portions thereof, may not be reproduced by any means without permission of the author.

ISBN-13: 978-1-944089-15-3

Praise for *Restless Bones*

"Marella Sands has a keen eye for detail, and an ability to take innocent research and bits of trivia, and turn them into stories that will disturb, frighten, charm, and make you think." Laurell K. Hamilton

"I think Marella Sands may have made a horror short-story fan out of me!" Kaylee Stevens

"Haunting and engrossing, this compilation of tales of spine-tingling horror will have you on the edge of your seat." Brenda Maxwell

"The stories are a great length to read in one sitting—if you can take it! I had goose bumps throughout." Nicole Hastings

"A must read for fans of horror and dark fantasy." Stacy Decker

"I was pleasantly surprised by the top-notch professionalism in this book, from the strength of the narration to the engaging storylines—a real challenge considering the shorter length of these stories. Kudos to Ms. Sands; she will be on my list of authors to watch." Max Gilbert

Praise for *Pandora's Mirror*

"This was a brilliant novel and very well-crafted. I was most impressed with the amazing writing—literary, beautiful, almost poetic prose that made the story even creepier to read." Essie Harmon

"The writing is simply lovely, with literary prose that has powerful, evocative word choices that truly bring this terrifying story to life. A fast read with shocking twists, and a satisfying ending." Nicole Hastings

"Warning—when starting Pandora's Mirror, *make sure you don't have anywhere you need to be or anything you need to do because you won't want to stop reading until you've finished it all!"* Stacy Decker

1

"The Fright House of Fenton" looked anything but scary.

In fact, from the outside, the two-story McMansion looked like every other house on the street: beige with white trim, two-car garage, well-manicured lawn. Completely unremarkable. Except no family had managed to spend more than a few nights here and real estate agents had given up on it.

Why my boss wanted me to look into a haunted house was a mystery. I'd given up trying to make sense of the world once I'd realized the supernatural existed, so I accepted there could be something unexplainable in the house that was scary enough to keep people out. I just didn't know why it was any of my business to be here.

"Kind of disappointing to look at," said Castro. He had decided that, if I were going to be involved in the supernatural, he was going to be, too. After all, two supernatural creatures had nearly cut his heart out about a month ago, so I guess he was entitled to get in the middle of everything with eyes wide open.

He'd always been someone who liked things like stories about Bigfoot and TV shows about ghost hunting. It was *me* that had never been interested, and now it was *me* that was involved in a lot of shit I'd rather not think about.

I unlocked the front door and walked right in. Castro followed a bit more slowly.

The interior was as tan and dull as the outside. I entered the large kitchen. It had stainless steel appliances, red granite countertops, an island with room for four barstools along one side, and even an overhead rack for hanging pots.

Not that there were any pots on it now. I doubt anyone had stayed long enough to unpack the boxes marked *kitchen*.

Castro was reading off his phone. "Three bedrooms upstairs, one on the main floor. Two and a half baths, laundry room off the garage. Full basement, framed in, not finished."

"Yeah, I saw the listing."

He looked up from the glowing screen and slowly scanned the open-plan first floor. "I've never lived in anything close to this. This is..."

"Pretentious?"

"I was going to say, ostentatious. But you beat me with your ten dollar word."

"They're both ten dollar words."

"But you said yours first." He smiled and leaned over to kiss me on the cheek. "Now, where shall we set up?"

I put down the duffel bag I'd lugged into the house. "I have no idea. This is your area."

"My area of interest, maybe, but not expertise. When is the expert going to get here?"

"I don't know. I don't even know who Ware is sending."

Ware was my boss, and one of the people I'd met who'd revealed he used to be some kind of ex-winged, mythological-type being now stuck on earth. Why Ware had any interest in this house was something he had failed to explain. He had also failed to say anything about who would be helping us, except to say to expect "someone."

My money was on that "someone" to be another ex-winged creature.

Not like my life was getting weird or anything.

"Can you sense anything?" asked Castro.

"What am I, a ghost detector now?"

Castro just unzipped the duffel bag. "Look, I have no idea what you can do, but Ware and the others keep saying you're somebody special. So...I dunno. *Are* you a ghost detector?"

"I don't believe in ghosts."

Castro glared at me.

"All right, I don't believe in the sort of ordinary, clomp down the hallway, orbs-in-photos kind of ghost. Clearly, fallen angels, or at least the things that started the stories about angels, exist. And...whatever it is that Ware keeps in the back." I shuddered. I hadn't taken a close look, but something that looked and smelled a bit like a pile of old leaves had scuttled around my feet the one time I'd been in Ware's private office. I didn't really want to know what it was, because I suspected I wouldn't like the answer.

"He wanted you along for a reason. Assuming he has your best interests at heart, and I'm not sure that he does, but, hey, let's say he does, then you're supposed to be an asset and you're not in any danger."

I didn't say anything to that. What was there to say? I wasn't sure Ware had my best interests at heart, either, and he was the one who was the most likely to be on my side.

"Of course, if hauntings aren't real, no one's in danger," I said.

"I'll go along with the part about your standard-issue hauntings probably aren't real," said Castro, "but something has scared a lot of people out of this house. And we are among the few people who know there really *are* supernatural things living, or existing, or whatever, in St. Louis. So, sure, this might not be what most people think of as a haunting, but I'm absolutely sure it's not nothing."

"Comforting." Which, of course, it was not.

"Let's check around the house since the expert's not here yet."

I shrugged. Might as well. We were stuck here for a weekend, at least, so we should know the layout of the home.

I headed for the stairs, but Castro stopped me with a laugh. "Seriously? Everything supposedly happens in the basement."

Now it was my turn to glare at him. Why would I want to go to the basement? On the other hand, what did it matter? I'd have to eventually.

Here for a weekend, at least. Yep. Cue the big sigh and the regret that I'd ever agreed to this.

"Fine," I said. "Let's check out the basement."

The stairs to the basement were on the far side of the kitchen. Castro went down first and I followed. He took a camera with him.

"We're not even set up yet and you're already taking pictures?"

"Why not? I want to *do* something. You know, *investigate.*"

That was so foreign to me. I just wanted to go home, look in on our pet hedgehog Petunia, and watch a movie. Those days were exceedingly rare, because my bartending job kept me out most evenings. Thus, it was always a treat when Castro and I could just do something for ourselves in our apartment, and lock the world outside, where it belonged.

This ghost hunting expedition was ruining that for me, and I resented it.

The basement was partially finished, as the listing said. To my right were the bare essentials: 2x4s affixed together. To my left, someone had managed to get up a few panels of drywall so there was at least one full room down here. Or maybe two. It was hard to tell from the bottom of the stairs.

"Exciting," I said.

Castro laughed. "You might sound bored, but I bet you're just a little intrigued."

Suddenly, I heard footsteps upstairs. I froze. No one had mentioned phantom footsteps in the house. Ware had only said stuff about sobbing in the basement and doors that opened themselves. A creepy feeling crept up my spine and I shivered.

"Hey, where are you guys?" shouted the squeaky voice of Castro's friend Andre.

I relaxed. "Downstairs." I glared at Castro. "You didn't say he was coming." Although, actually, I was relieved. I had been wondering how Castro and I could possibly watch the house and record data for forty-eight hours straight without someone to spell us. Now we had Andre. I was just a little put out that Castro hadn't said anything.

Castro shrugged. "I didn't actually think he was coming. He was interested, but then he said he had other things to do."

That made sense. Andre was capable of finding a date whenever he wanted, but, so far, was incapable of finding second dates. That had always struck me as a little weird; Andre seemed like a perfectly nice guy. So why couldn't he find someone? The upshot was that his schedule tended to be unpredictable and his attendance at social events was sporadic.

Andre thudded down the stairs; even though he was a string bean, he always walked as though he weighed three hundred pounds. Surprisingly, he was followed by a hollow-cheeked girl with screaming red hair and a mass of tattoos down each arm. She also sported a nose ring and lots of dark make-up that made her skin look sallow.

"Hi," said Andre. "This is my cousin Brooklyn from Las Vegas. She's staying with me for a little while." The look on Andre's face was a combination of embarrassment, presumably for foisting this cousin on us, and annoyance, possibly because "a little while" had already been longer than he'd like.

"Hi," said Castro. Of the two of us, he was the more outgoing, and he also had a deep-seated need to make others comfortable in awkward situations. He claimed that was because he'd spent far too much time in foster homes where everyone spent their days walking on eggshells.

Andre stepped into the basement and looked around nervously. He rubbed his chin, where I spotted the beginnings of a goatee. "Any weird stuff yet?"

"We just got here," said Castro. He walked up to Brooklyn and extended his right hand. "Welcome to our little weekend experiment in the paranormal."

Brooklyn's sour face took on a slightly more relaxed cast and she shook Castro's hand.

"I'm Castro," he said, "and this is Teryl."

I nodded to Brooklyn, and she actually smiled a little. I got the feeling she hadn't been genuinely welcomed by anyone for a long time. But, hey, if she could help work the equipment and take some late night or early evening shifts to let me get some sleep, I was all for having another assistant.

"Have you ever done something like this before?" asked Castro.

Brooklyn shook her head. "Nah. I haven't even watched those ghost hunting shows Andre likes."

"She won't watch a scary movie," said Andre with a frown. "I can't show her all my favorites."

I knew Andre's favorites included some all-time classics as *Night of the Living Dead*, but also clunkers like *Killer Klowns from Outer Space*. Andre's taste might best be summed up by the fact that he liked both versions of *The Wicker Man*, which shouldn't be humanly possible.

"OK," I said. "We probably ought to start setting up what little equipment we have."

Brooklyn froze, her eyes suddenly focused on a spot just behind me. "What's that?"

Slowly, I turned. Castro had already snapped a couple of pictures.

The half-done drywall was all I saw. "Dunno," I said.

"I saw something," Brooklyn insisted. "I swear, there was something there."

"I believe you," I said.

"You don't," she said. "No one ever does."

I turned back to her; her eyes were now staring at her feet. She lifted her gaze to me slowly, a look of defiance on her face.

"I said I believe you, and I do," I said. "I was told by someone who knows about these things that there's something here. Maybe you're more sensitive to it than me."

Brooklyn visibly relaxed. That made me wonder about the "no one ever does" comment. Did this girl think she was a psychic or something?

Andre shifted his weight awkwardly. "Um, Brooklyn sees a lot of things."

Okay, psychic. Or something.

Brooklyn shot him an angry glance, but before she could say anything, the doorbell rang. Andre nearly jumped out of his skin. Brooklyn looked like she might faint.

"Doorbell. Just a doorbell," said Castro. "That's probably the expert that's supposed to show."

Brooklyn and Andre fled up the stairs, with me and Castro close behind. I went to the front door and opened it.

Staring at me was indeed one of those ex-winged supernatural creatures like my boss. This one looked like a refugee from Woodstock with shapeless clothing and long straight darkly brown hair. What truly stood out about her was her eyes. They were a stunning green, making the frumpiness of the rest of her appearance fade from one's consciousness. Her eyes would catch yours and hold on and everything else became unimportant.

She might not be an actual angel, only something inhuman that helped found the legends of angels, but that didn't mean she didn't have a certain ability to compel the attention of the humans around her, even with the ridiculous hippie ensemble.

"Hi, Lucy," I said. "Welcome to the Fright House."

2

"This hardly looks like the kind of place that sports a ghost," said Lucy as she slipped inside. She had a shapeless bag with her which appeared to be empty, and otherwise, she carried no supplies or equipment.

"Ware said he was sending an expert," I said. "I guess that's you?"

Lucy shrugged. "We're all experts of a sort," she said. "But you wouldn't want Fish or Oya on a job like this. And Yama would just try to poison the thing."

That left out the other supernatural creature in my boss's drinking buddies group: Truck. I knew nothing about him except he looked like a stereotypical redneck. Just as Lucy looked very stereotypically flower child-like, and Fish resembled a down-on-his luck drunken sot. As if these creatures either picked stereotypes to disappear into, or they were the basis for them to begin with.

The thought made my head hurt. I didn't care what they were, only that they were fucking up my life a little bit at a time.

Andre came from behind me. "Found the kitchen," he said. "There's no food. I can go out and get some." He caught sight of Lucy. "Oh, hi. Are you the psychic?"

"Expert," said Lucy tartly. "I'm hardly psychic."

"Oh," said Andre. He shrugged. "I guess we need an expert. Did you bring any equipment? I can fetch it from your car."

Lucy plastered a wide but insincere smile on her face. She had always seemed enigmatic; now she just seemed condescending. "No need," she said. "I was dropped off. I don't have any equipment to bring in."

"Oh," said Andre again. "Okay. Well, Brooklyn should be able to help us with the psychic stuff. She just doesn't like to."

"Unusual gifts can be quite uncomfortable to bear," said Lucy. She walked by me. "You say the kitchen's back here?"

"Yeah, sure," said Andre. He watched Lucy go, then turned to me. "Who's that again? She's an odd one."

If he only knew how odd.

"Lucy," I said. "One of my boss's friends."

"Your boss who owns the bar?" Andre didn't drink and had never been to my place of work. He had only a vague notion of where it was and what I did there. Sometimes, I got the feeling he pictured a high-class place filled with people in tuxedos and wearing shiny shoes, when the reality was more like forgotten people sporting worn clothing and downcast expressions. A lot of them could stand to be introduced to body wash and shampoo.

Castro came from the dining room, and pointed back toward the area. "Hey, if you're not too busy, come help with the stuff. And, Teryl, why don't you and Brooklyn go around the house to get some baseline readings."

"Baseline readings on what?" I asked.

"EMF meter. Try to get an EVP or two. Go to every room. If there's a couple of places that seem colder than others, or where the EMF meter goes crazy, then we know what areas are the top priority for the cameras. We don't have enough to cover the whole house."

The jargon irritated me. EMF meter? EVP?

Brooklyn came into the room; now that we were in a better-lit area, it was obvious she was related to Andre. She was pale with wavy hair and he was darker with tightly-curled hair, but they had a certain way of standing, of walking. In movement, they were more like brother and sister than cousin.

The important thing was that Brooklyn had a small electronic device in each hand. She held one out to me.

"Here's the EMF meter," she said. "Just turn it on and see how many of the lights blink. In some areas of the house, there probably won't be any. In others, the lights might go crazy."

"And that's supposed to detect ghosts?" I stared at the little box dubiously.

"Not really," said Andre. "It just lets you know if there's something going on in the electromagnetic bands. So unshielded wiring will make it go off, too. Other electronic devices. Probably pacemakers and shit like that."

"So I'm looking for electromagnetism in a world full of electrical wiring and Wi-Fi," I said. "Won't it just go off all the time for perfectly normal reasons?"

"Yes," said Brooklyn. "The idea is to see if there are certain areas of the house where it goes off more. It gives us a way to prioritize where to put cameras and stuff."

Whatever. I nodded to what she was holding. "And that?"

"Just a recorder. For EVP."

I couldn't help but roll my eyes and she looked abashed. "Electronic voice phenomenon. We ask questions and see if we get any responses."

I wanted to be cynical about that as well, but hearing her say that sent a shiver up my spine. Or maybe down my spine. It made me shudder, anyway.

"Okay, let's do this," I said. "Where do we start?"

"It's a two-story house," she said. "Let's start upstairs and work our way down."

The stairs were to my left. Pale off-white carpet coated them, furthering the bland off-white and beige color palette of the house. Did no one in McMansionland like color?

"Turn on the meter, and go first," said Brooklyn. "If the lights start to go crazy at any point, let me know and I'll turn on the recorder."

"Fine." I headed up the steps, holding the doodad in front of me. At the top of the steps a light blinked. That didn't seem to meet the requirement of "going crazy," so I dismissed it and went on.

The second floor contained two small bedrooms, a bathroom at the end of the hall, and a master suite that included an en suite bathroom. The en suite bathroom was probably three or four hundred square feet. It contained two sinks, a separate tub and shower, a toilet, a large closet which contained a washer and dryer, and bay window complete with a window seat.

Who wanted to go into the bathroom to sit in a window nook? I assumed the window seat was due to someone deciding to do *something* with the oddly-shaped room. Something to make the bizarre bay window area look functional rather than lonely and empty.

The meter occasionally blessed me with a spark of light, but nothing exciting.

"Well, let's go downstairs," said Brooklyn. She sounded disappointed. Then she stopped. "Wait, let's try an EVP just in case." She stood in the hallway in front of the master suite doorway, held the recorder in front of her, and said, "Is anyone here?" She waited a few seconds, then added. "Do you have a name?" More questions followed, at intervals clearly designed to allow something to answer if it so chose. "Is anyone with you? Are you trapped here? Is there something we can do for you?"

After a while, she turned off the recorder. "Okay, now we'll try downstairs."

At the bottom of the steps, we met Lucy, who now had a glass of wine in her hand. White wine, which surprised me a bit. Ware and his companions normally drank harder stuff, but when they got a wine bottle out, it was always red. I guess Lucy could indulge a personal preference once out of Ware's presence.

"Trying out some EVP," she said. It wasn't a question. "Hope you get something. That's always interesting."

"I don't think I've ever gotten anything with EVP," said Brooklyn, "but I always hope I will."

Lucy cocked her head in a friendly manner. "How many of these sort of investigations have you been on?"

"Just a couple, at least organized ones where a group went. But alone, I've tried EVPs in cemeteries, old churches, abandoned buildings...basically anywhere I think I might find a spirit hanging out."

"Do spirits just *hang out*?" I asked Lucy. She was a supernatural creature; if anyone were going to know, it would be her.

"What an interesting question," said Lucy. I thought she sounded sarcastic, but I wasn't sure. I didn't know her, but it was easy to believe that a creature like her might be simultaneously amused and annoyed by questions from mere mortals like myself. After all, they had to hear the same questions generation after generation, right? "In my experience, only certain people get to *hang out* after death. But others may go off and have different fates. Not everyone is lucky enough to stay at home and get asked questions by nosy young people with digital recorders and ghost boxes."

"Ah, damn, we don't have a ghost box," said Castro as he approached from the direction of the dining room. "I knew there was something I was forgetting."

"Do you even own one of these things?" I asked. I'd never heard him mention a ghost box. But then, I didn't recall any discussions about EMF meters, either, and I was holding one of those at this very moment.

"No, no, but I got a little money last week for doing all Mrs. Raymond's chores. I was going to use that to buy one."

"I guess you can slate that money for something else," I said. "Some food for Petunia, maybe."

"Petunia?" asked Brooklyn.

"Our pet hedgehog," said Castro proudly. "She and Teryl are my sweet ladies."

Lucy shook her head; her heavy dark hair swayed around her shoulders. "Well, I heard you upstairs asking questions. See if you got anything."

Brooklyn started the recorder and we all listened to her voice say *Is anyone here?*

The recording continued; I was embarrassed to hear myself in the background making a choking sound. I realized I had been trying not to laugh out loud.

Castro shot me a look that said he knew what I'd been trying to not do. I just shrugged helplessly. This entire situation had *theater of the absurd* written all over it.

I actually wasn't quite sure what that phrase meant, but it truly seemed to apply here.

Brooklyn's voice stopped and the recorder hadn't captured anything but the two of us. Then, just before she turned it off, Lucy held up her hand. "There. Play that back."

I hadn't heard anything, but I'd trust that Lucy had keen hearing. My boss certainly did and they were of the same species.

Brooklyn played back the last few seconds of the recording. Now I heard a soft hiss that I could swear had not been there in the hall when we'd been standing there.

"What was that?" asked Castro. "Just a sound? A word? I couldn't tell."

"Turn it up," said Lucy. "I think we'll hear it more clearly then."

I took that to mean that she, with her supernatural hearing, already knew what the hiss was, but she was pretending to have human-level hearing around the mere mortals in the room.

Brooklyn played the bit back again. This time, the message was clearer. Just before the recording ended, a very faint voice, like that of a small child, hissed *help*.

My heart nearly stopped. Something invisible had talked to the recorder. A wave of dizziness passed over me. I found myself scratching the oddly-shaped scar on the palm of my right hand. When I realized what I was doing, I stopped.

I looked over at Lucy, who seemed inordinately pleased, as if she had just gotten confirmation of something she'd suspected but hadn't been sure of.

Brooklyn's eyes got wide. Castro slapped a hand over his mouth in glee.

"Oh, my god," said Brooklyn. "We've got ourselves a ghost."

.

3

"There's nothing quite like your first ghost hunt," said Andre with a wry smile. He had returned from his run to the grocery store to the news of the EVP, and was both giddy with excitement that we'd captured evidence of the paranormal already, and disappointed he hadn't been here with us when it happened.

I was already tired of it, actually, but I smiled, too. Lucy gave me a knowing smile as if she knew what I were thinking.

My gut froze for a moment. She might actually know what I was thinking. Fish, the ragged sot who drank constantly, was one of these creatures, the Forlorn, and he could read thoughts.

Actually, he couldn't avoid them, if you listened to him, unless he had enough alcohol on board. Then the thoughts of the humans in his vicinity were masked enough that he could ignore them. He claimed he had no interest in the thoughts of others, and considering how much alcohol he put away every day, I had to believe him.

Maybe Lucy could read minds, too. She walked by me, shook her head slightly, and whispered, "Only Fish."

When I gave her a look of alarm, she muttered, "I can read faces just fine, dear, and you are an open book."

"I got a pizza in the oven," said Castro. "So dinner in twenty. Then you guys can finish the EVPs around the house."

"Why not finish them now?" asked Brooklyn. She seemed energized now having had a bit of success.

"If you want, sure," said Castro. "I'd like to be along, though, and I've got to make the salad."

"I can do that," I said, thinking that here was my chance to get off of ghost detail.

Castro frowned, no doubt distrusting my lack of ability in the kitchen.

"It comes in a bag, doesn't it?" I asked. "All I have to do is slice up the onions and tomatoes and add them to it, right? I think I can do that. I can probably even do it and not cut myself with the knife."

Which, for me, would be an accomplishment. But, while Castro would know that, no one else had to.

"All right," he said. It was a measure of how badly he wanted to do this ghost hunt that he was willing to abandon me to kitchen duty.

I went to the kitchen and found a knife to open the salad bag with. I poured out the greens into a bowl and started chopping on the onion.

Lucy joined me. That made me a little nervous; well, truthfully, my boss and all of his friends made me nervous. Except Fish. Fish was pitiful, not frightening. The others, though, were people I'd been wary of even before I found out what they were.

"Ware didn't tell you much about this, did he?" Lucy asked without preamble. She must be confident none of the others was within earshot. Well, she would know. She was the one with the supernatural senses.

"Not a lot," I said. "I'm not even sure why he's interested. Surely, you guys can't care so much about dead humans."

"Oh, mostly we're not," she said dismissively. "Most of you simply fade out when you die. Like, you might exist independent of your mortal remains for a few minutes, and then, you just dissolve."

"So there aren't ghosts?" I asked.

"I said *most of you*. The rest...have a different fate."

I remembered Marco Kendall in the alley, and the perfume-laden thing Oya had flung at Marveaux in the crypt under Bellefontaine Cemetery.

"I know," I whispered. I could recall consuming Kendall's soul, as if it were a meal. I didn't mean I literally chewed it and swallowed it, but I'd wrapped my arms around his frantic ghost and had simply absorbed him. Later, I'd used his energy to win my fight against Marveaux. Just thinking how I'd used Kendall and destroyed him made me nauseated. I hadn't known what I was doing, but I was still guilty of that destruction. Marco Kendall had been murdered, had turned into a frightened spirit, and then had been absorbed and shredded into oblivion. He hadn't deserved any of it.

I didn't even know how I'd done what I'd done, or how I could keep it from happening again. When I'd seen Kendall in the alley, it had been as if I'd been compelled to embrace him and absorb his energy into myself. Why had I felt like that? I didn't know.

"The thing..." I whispered. "The thing in Ware's office." I couldn't even look at Lucy when I said it.

"Oh, that." She shrugged. "We call them scraps. They're sometimes what's left of a person after they die."

"Sometimes?"

A noise came from the basement. I froze mid-slice down the onion. Lucy's eyes glittered with something like excitement.

"So, have you been down there?" she asked. "What's in the basement?"

"Not much," I said. "Some half-finished walls. Some trash."

"Huh."

"Are you looking for something in particular?"

She just smiled. "I'm always on the lookout for something."

"For Ware?"

That made her smile falter. "What do you know of it?"

My eyes were burning from the onion. Stupid of me to take on kitchen duty for multiple reasons, right? I pushed the damn thing away from me and picked up a tomato. Much less dangerous.

"Not much," I said. "Well, basically, nothing. I know that stupid key that kept appearing around me led to something Ware wanted. A pink rock. Oya said something about Ware sending her on assignments to find things. So, if she has those kinds of jobs to do for Ware, maybe you do, too."

Lucy relaxed. "Oh. No, I don't do those kinds of errands. Little Girl will," she said, using the name for Oya that Ware and his other drinking buddies used. As Oya was well over six feet tall, the name didn't suit her. I assumed it was supposed to be a joke.

"Fish mentioned you all have different talents," I said. "So is that why you're here? He can read minds and you can..." I trailed off, hoping she'd fill in the blanks. I'd heard once that she had some kind of affinity for water, but I had no idea what that meant.

"I certainly can't read minds," she said. "And am grateful for it. Look what it's done to poor Fish."

Another thump from downstairs. Lucy leaned back toward the living room of the house. "Hey, ghost hunters, seems like the basement is a good place to go right now!"

In less than ten seconds, the rest of the crew was there in the kitchen. Castro looked at me, eyebrows asking a question.

"Thumping from downstairs," I said. "Go get 'em."

Castro grinned and headed for the steps, Brooklyn and Andre just behind him.

"They're so cute," said Lucy as they disappeared down the stairs.

The condescension was thick. "Look, I know you're from some other species, all immortal and supernatural and what-not, but do you have to be a jerk like that?" I asked. "It's not like you guys are doling out ancient wisdom or answers to life's questions. We have to go looking on our own if we want to learn anything. From what I can see, you guys mostly drink and look down on us."

That made her grin and finished her wine. "Yeah, I can see your point on that, and it's not the first time, or the hundredth, that someone's said the exact same words to me. So pardon me if I don't get all weepy and contrite."

For the first time, I wondered where she'd gotten the wine. Andre had said there'd been no food in the house, and she hadn't arrived with a bottle. I guess she'd found some in the pantry or in a cabinet.

Of course, just because Andre had said he hadn't found food didn't mean he considered *wine* under the category *food*. Maybe he'd found an entire stash of alcohol somewhere and then Lucy had found it as well. He still would have wanted to stock the fridge with actual, you know, *food*.

I finished with the tomato and dumped the slimy bits into the greens. I added what I had chopped of the onion. A little of that stuff goes a long way, especially with an onion as powerful as this one.

I checked on the pizza. It seemed to be cooking well, with the crust beginning to look a little toasty. Pepperoni. Of course. I didn't understand the relationship between young men and pepperoni pizza, but it certainly seemed as if all of them preferred that to any other kind. Castro gravitated toward pepperoni every chance he got; I generally had to speak up early or buy my own pizza if I wanted hamburger or onions or mushrooms on mine.

"What's in the basement?" I asked.

"I don't know," said Lucy. "I only know what I hope it is."

"A scrap?"

Lucy grinned and pulled a bottle of wine out of the refrigerator. Along with of a few things like eggs and bags of greens, that were near the front of the shelves, the fridge contained several bottles of wine and at least a few cans of beer. I briefly wondered how old the stuff was and resolved not to drink it. Let Lucy down it all.

"Maybe," she said at last.

"And would that be a good thing?"

She poured herself more wine and this time, left the bottle on the counter. I guess she planned to finish it before leaving the kitchen.

"Depends on your point of view," she said. "Are you hoping the scrap gets a long and happy afterlife? Because I'm guessing you must realize by now that isn't going to happen."

I closed my eyes briefly, the dizziness I felt around Lucy and Ware passing over me once more. "So, we humans can dissolve into nothingness, or become *scraps* that exist for some time after death, but ultimately, are miserable and short-lived?"

She looked thoughtful and took a swig of the wine. "Something like that. Guess I could have tried to sugar-coat it a bit, but ultimately, it is what it is."

"And Ware keeps one for what, as a pet?"

"You could say that."

"What else could I say," I muttered, becoming more annoyed by her evasiveness.

"You could say he keeps it to use it someday. Just because it's a scrap doesn't mean it has no value."

"Value. As a weapon? An item of trade? A meal?"

"Those things are not mutually exclusive," she said.

We were interrupted by a whoop from downstairs. It sounded like Castro.

"Bingo!" he was saying.

Someone ran up the steps. It was indeed Castro. "Hey, Teryl, you'll never believe what we found down there!" He glanced in dismay at the oven, which was now emitting a wisp of smoke. "Oh, crap, did you burn the pizza?"

Lucy laughed and took both wineglass and bottle into another room. Red-faced, I opened the oven and removed the pizza. The perimeter of the crust had turned black but otherwise, it seemed okay.

"It's still edible," I said. "So, what did you find?"

4

The pizza was devoured as if locusts had descended on the house. Somehow, Andre, Castro, and Brooklyn were so fired up they managed to talk and tell me about all the bangs and cold spots in the basement without pausing and also, miraculously, choking.

I barely got one piece of the pizza; by the time I was finished with that, the others had consumed the rest. I remembered that Andre had also bought some cheese and crackers and decided that would be my real dinner. That and the salad no one had touched so far.

We ate in the living room, where a way-too-soft couch and loveseat set were gathered around a glass coffee table. The little bit of equipment Castro had brought was on the dining room table and no one wanted to move it just to have to move it back after eating.

Lucy wandered the house and ate nothing, as far as I could tell. I've seen Fish eat, so I know the Forlorn *can* eat. I just don't know if they *have to*.

She did finish off the bottle of wine.

Andre slid the EVP recorder onto the coffee table. "Here, listen to this," he said.

At first, all I heard was the sound of various footfalls, which did not excite the others at the table, so I assume those were their own steps. Then Castro said, "Isn't the basement where most things are supposed to have happened?"

"I'm sensing something," said Brooklyn. "I get a feeling we need to go toward that corner over there. Something is watching us, but it's not violent. At least, I'm not getting anger or hate."

"How do you tell the difference?" asked Castro.

Brooklyn's answer was a bit muffled, but I could still hear her say, "When they're angry, you *know*. Like, you feel like you want to puke. What I'm picking up now is making me feel a little sad, but not ill."

"Sad?" asked Andre. "Like, it's sad, or you're sad?"

"Not sure there's a difference," said Brooklyn softly. She had clearly moved away from Castro, who had the recorder.

Okay, so now I knew what Brooklyn figured constituted a psychic power: she could sense presences and know if they were angry or not. I guess that was useful. If Lucy were right, though, most humans simply dissipated after death, so there really shouldn't be anything for Brooklyn to pick up on for the vast majority of the population.

I guess saying human souls dissolved after the death of the body didn't really answer the question of, did they dissolve into oblivious, or did they then go somewhere else. Like, did they "dissolved" in the same way that *Star Trek* characters "beamed" from one place to another. Not instantaneously, but over a few seconds?

My feeling was that Lucy had no idea and that made me wonder if she'd ever even thought about the issue. Maybe she and the other Forlorn simply assumed that human souls dissolved into nothingness, and they were wrong.

They might be some kind of star-traveling species, or at least they had been at one time, but that didn't mean they were always right about everything. They were still beings, not gods. Powerful beings, but fallible like any other creature. In a way, I found that comforting. I might be in the middle of some kind of power struggle between Forlorn factions, but at least they weren't all-powerful or all-knowing. *More* powerful and *more* knowing than humans, but not infinitely so.

As far as I was concerned, that meant I just might live through whatever fight Fish and Ware saw coming.

The light falling on the table from outside was blotted out for a moment. I looked over, but saw nothing but the boring flat back yard of this property. You'd think someone would have planted a tree, or put out a bench, or at least hung up a wind chime, or *something*. Instead, the property consisted of the house and its driveway and street-side mailbox, and grass.

Boring. Suburban. Plain. Nothing to make you think there could be anything vaguely interesting going on inside or outside.

I assumed the light had been blocked by a bird flying by, and focused again on the recording.

"Is anyone here?" asked Castro.

After a few moments, Brooklyn said something, but she was far enough away from Castro that it sounded as though she mumbled the question. But I thought she said, "I can feel you. Are you sad?" or something very similar.

A hiss came onto the recorder and a quiet word. I sounded like *don't*.

Castro spoke again, "Are you lost? Are you trying to move on?"

Nothing to that.

Brooklyn again, this time louder. "Are you the one who asked for help? Or is there more than one entity here?"

More hissing, and another *don't*. But this utterance was slightly longer. Maybe *don't get* or *don't let*.

"Did you see that?" asked Andre on the recorder. The Andre sitting on the loveseat nodded vigorously and said, "I saw a shadow move in the corner." He held up his phone. "Didn't get a photo;

moved too fast. But I'm going to set up one of the cameras tonight in the basement and have it record that corner."

"Shut up," said Castro. "I think we had another EVP response." He moved the recording back a few seconds.

The voice was back, still quiet, still saying *don't* but this time it sounded like *don't let them in.*

"Don't let them in?" asked Brooklyn. "Who's *them?*"

I shot a glance at Lucy, but she appeared bored and was staring into the kitchen, no doubt contemplating grabbing another bottle of wine.

"I don't know," said Castro. "But I guess we're dealing with more than one entity here. One that wants help, and at least two that want to get inside the house? I mean, if it's really saying *don't let them in,* then there has to be more than one something that's trying to get in here."

"It might not mean the house," said Brooklyn. "It might mean the basement, or even the metaphysical space it's currently occupying. I mean, we don't really know where it thinks it is or how much it understands what it is, or what happened to it, or what it's doing here."

"I don't think it means the house," said Lucy, as if she'd finally noticed the conversation swirling around her. "I don't know where this thing thinks it is, but wherever that it, it thinks it's alone there, and it's afraid more might join it."

"Join it in this house?" asked Andre.

Lucy appeared bored again. "Join it wherever it thinks it is. Not necessarily this house, because we don't even know that it's aware of this plane of existence. For all we know, it thinks it's a real person who's hearing the voices of the dead ask it questions."

"That's a mind-fuck," said Andre. He shook his head. "Well, at least we know we're alive and it's not."

"Do we?" asked Lucy with a half-smile. "Now, excuse me while I get something more to drink."

"Hell, for all we know," said Castro, "it *is* a living a person, just in another dimension or something. How do we even determine that it's a ghost. I mean, what is that, really?"

"A dead person, obviously," said Andre.

"Is it so obvious?" asked Castro. "Think about this: what if it's a time-traveling dog from the future who's stuck in some vortex it can't get out of?"

This was starting to sound like Fish's quantum mechanics explanation of hauntings. I guess he and Castro had discussed the idea at some point.

"Dogs bark," said Andre.

"They do now," said Castro. "Maybe dogs from the future have been genetically modified to talk like people?"

"That's stupid," said Brooklyn.

Castro shrugged. "Maybe. All I'm saying is, with the data we have, we can't tell the difference between a dead human being and a time-traveling talking dog. Literally, we cannot tell."

"Then let's go with dead human," said Andre. "No need to complicate things."

"No need to label it at all," said Castro. "That's what I'm saying. We have a voice on the recorder. Maybe a shadow. From the stories about this place, there will probably also be some weird noises tonight. That much we can document. What, exactly, is making those sounds and saying those words and casting those shadows is just a guess on our part."

"What if it tells us it's a dead person?" asked Andre.

"What if it's lying?" I said, sticking myself into the conversation for the first time. "Or what if it's not lying but it's mistaken? How can you determine which is which?"

Brooklyn shook her head and ate the last bit of pizza she had been holding in her hand. It was probably cold as fuck by now, but she didn't seem to notice. "We can't. Which is fine, really. We want to label things, but do they really need labels?"

"Yes," said Andre and Castro at the same time.

A loud crash came from the basement.

"Lucy?" I shouted. "You okay?"

"I'm in the kitchen. I'm fine," she said. "But sounds like you need to check that out."

"I thought she was the expert," mumbled Andre. "Why isn't she rushing downstairs?"

Andre and Castro left the room. I glanced over at Brooklyn, but she rolled her eyes. "Let them be the heroes and go check out the loud noises. I'm just as glad to stay up here and not be around something so damn sad. I hate crying."

"Me, too," I said. I sighed and glanced at the dining room. "I think I know how to set up Castro's stuff, so I can do a little bit to be useful. You want to help?"

"Sure," said Brooklyn. "It beats watching the shadows."

I had no idea what she meant by that and decided not to ask. We went into the dining room, where Castro had carefully, but chaotically, set down his stuff. A pile of cables had been dumped onto the floor.

I started sorting through everything and handed Brooklyn one cable after another. "Camera. Computer. Charger," I said, pointing to the appropriate device. Brooklyn started getting everything attached to the power strip that Castro had already plugged into the wall. Overall, just getting equipment ready to go was easy enough. Definitely something I could accomplish, unlike cooking a pizza.

A shadow moved around the room and I looked up. Brooklyn froze.

"It's here," she said.

"I don't know," I said. "I think it came from outside. Probably a neighbor or something." I looked out the window; this one faced the street. The driveway held my car Nixie, and Andre's beat-up Aveo. From my vantage point, I saw several people walking dogs, one jogger, and one white car driving away toward the main street. The view from the dining room was pure dull Americana.

Nothing unusual. Nothing that could have made a shadow.

Brooklyn glanced at the neighborhood and seemed slightly triumphant. "It's definitely something in here with us. But at least it seems timid. We should be able to record it if it sticks around, but it doesn't seem like it's strong enough to harm us."

"If it's alone here," I said. "We still don't know who this mysterious *them* is."

Someone, or something, knocked on the front door. I froze. So did Brooklyn. I hadn't seen anyone come up the driveway.

Brooklyn shook her head. "It can't be a person. Stay here. Don't answer it."

I was in agreement. If someone had really walked up to the door, we would have seen them. After all, we had just been looking outside. Like, five seconds ago. It wasn't like we were in the middle of a forest where someone could approach the front of the house under cover or something.

Lucy came out of the kitchen. "I kinda like this place," she said. "Doesn't give you time to get bored between talking, knocking, or rustling around, does it?"

"Yeah," I said. "I guess so. It's an active haunted house."

Lucy laughed. "Ware wouldn't have sent you here if it weren't, or have asked me to join you. Even so, I hadn't expected anything quite this active. Tonight's going to be a good night, I think."

Lucy raised a glass to the two of us before returning to the kitchen. Brooklyn no longer appeared triumphant; rather, she was somewhat cowed. "Tonight. All night," she said. "Guess I won't be sleeping while I'm here."

I didn't figure some odd thumping would keep me up, not after the things I'd seen lately. But still, this house was creeping me out a bit. "Sure," I said. "Who needs sleep?"

5

In the end, we decided to take shifts. Castro insisted on getting some sleep first because he wanted to be up for the "witching hour" of 3:00 a.m. Apparently, my thought that the witching hour was midnight was incorrect; not only Castro, but Andre, Brooklyn, *and* Lucy all set me straight on that one.

So it was me, along with Brooklyn, who said she didn't plan to sleep at all, on the first shift. Castro and Andre laid out their sleeping bags on the living room floor and were soon out, if the deep breathing and occasional snore were any indications.

I have no idea if the Forlorn needed sleep, but Lucy didn't make any indication she planned to do anything but stay awake, though she didn't officially volunteer for a shift. So far, it wasn't clear to me why Ware had sent her along, but I had a sneaking feeling the empty cross body bag she never took off was actually why she was here.

Lucy only went in the kitchen now to refill her wine glass. By the fourth or fifth glass, Brooklyn gave me a questioning look, and I just shrugged. I could hardly explain that Lucy was a supernatural creature who couldn't get drunk. I'd just let Brooklyn assume Lucy was a hard-core drinker with a liver of steel, which was basically the truth, anyway.

I had eaten the salad and thrown down some cheddar cheese on Triscuits so at least my stomach wasn't making itself known anymore. I sat in front of the monitors showing the four feeds from the video cameras in the basement, living room, kitchen, and the master suite upstairs.

Brooklyn occasionally looked at the monitors, but mostly she glanced around nervously. This shift was going to be extremely long if she didn't loosen up.

"So, Lucy," I said, "you're the expert. You've got to have been to some interesting hauntings in the past. Why not give us a story?" I wanted to add *and keep Brooklyn's attention away from every shadow, creak, and whir of the monitors.*

"Oh, I could tell you about this brave knight who married a dragon and had many children by her. But he betrayed her in the end and she flew off and left him there in a crumbling castle, their children dead at his feet."

"Charming," I said. "Can't wait to hear it. But I was hoping for something a bit more relevant."

"Sounds awful," said Brooklyn. "What about a happy story?"

"Hauntings aren't happy," said Lucy. "But I'll try." She cocked her head slightly; her green eyes narrowed. "Well, how about this? Once upon a time, there were these brilliant beings, angels really, who came to earth because it was the most beautiful place they'd ever seen."

My ears perked up. Lucy was giving me some details about her own past, but couching it in a way that wouldn't cue Brooklyn in that these was for real. Still, for the life of me, I had no idea why Lucy would bother to tell me anything if Ware wouldn't. Ware played everything close to the chest, and had only dribbled out a tiny bit of information. Maybe Lucy would be less close-lipped, even if she were one of his drinking buddies.

"They loved the inhabitants of this planet, and tried to give them every gift they could imagine. The taming of fire, the secrets of agriculture, the invention of writing. They gave everything freely and were happy."

Considering how unhappy the Forlorn I'd met seemed to be, I wasn't quite buying this story so far, but I could hardly say that with Brooklyn in the room.

"That's nice," said Brooklyn.

"You'd think so. But two of the angels were more potent than the others, and the others flocked to one or the other. One faction wanted to leave humans alone as much as possible; the other wanted to take care of them forever. After all, the angels had taught humans about fire, and the humans burned each other to death with it. They had taught humans about crops, and the various tribes of humanity trampled each other's crops into the ground to starve their enemies. The beings had given humans writing so that their stories could be preserved, and the humans wrote lies. Kings exalted themselves with tales of magnificent tasks they had never undertaken, or shrouded themselves with glory that they had never attained. Everything the angels gave humans the humans turned to dust."

"The gifts were ours to do with as we wished," I said. "So some of us did bad things. That didn't make the gifts bad in and of themselves."

Lucy swirled the wine in her glass and shrugged.

"That was the first angel's thought, and why he wanted humans to learn on their own how to use the gifts wisely. It was the other, his brother, his closest friend, who wanted to control how humans used the gifts they had been given."

"Control freak," said Brooklyn. "Figures."

"So we've got one angel who's hands-off and another who's like an abusive father, or, maybe, pet owner," I said. I was thinking through the few Forlorn I knew, but Ware was the only one that seemed powerful enough to have been one of these figures. Which one, though? He seemed to fit the description of the hands-off angel more, but maybe he hadn't been like that originally and had changed over time.

"The two, who had been closer than any others, became mortal enemies," said Lucy. "There was a war. And one was cast down."

"Satan," said Brooklyn with a certain intensity. When Lucy shot her a look, Brooklyn said more meekly, "I mean, that's what I was taught."

"Satan is too small a concept for the beings I am describing," said Lucy.

"How did this all come about?" I asked.

"The two angels had been closer to brothers, as I said," Lucy continued, "and they agreed on one thing above all else: they loved the same woman. A being of their own kind. The most beautiful, most loved and most loving, most wise, and most compassionate of all of the angels. Both of them loved her beyond measure, which wasn't a problem before they had their falling out. But afterward, her heart was torn. In the war, she had to choose."

"Whom did she choose?" I asked, feeling the answer was going to matter to me very much if Ware turned out to be one of these two feuding brothers Lucy was describing.

"She chose the side that wanted humans to find their own path, even though it grieved her every time a human misused one of her gifts."

"What happened to her?" asked Brooklyn.

"She died," said Lucy flatly. The lack of emotion in her voice made me shiver. Ware had told me once that his kind could be killed but that it had only happened once. He hadn't elaborated, but his very reluctance to tell me about this woman's death surely meant he was one of the brothers who had loved her beyond reason.

"Each of her angel lovers blamed the other for her death. The war was even more terrible after that. Seas boiled. Mountains crumbled. Humans cried out in terror as their world remade itself."

"And then?" Brooklyn was really on the hook now.

I, on the other hand, was appalled. Was this what Ware saw coming? Was this why he thought I was special and protected me? Because the war was actually ongoing, and I had been recruited to serve without even knowing?

"The female angel had taken a human lover," said Lucy. "And had managed, through some feat of love and magic, to conceive a half-breed child with him."

"A lover?" Brooklyn was wide-eyed. "Who could love an angel?"

"The angel's lover has had many names in legend," said Lucy, "Gilgamesh is the name you may know best, but that was not his actual name."

"And their descendants?" I asked, giving Lucy a hard stare. She had decided to tell this for a reason, and I wanted her to say that out loud. She hadn't brought up the subject of a half-angel half-human baby because it was unimportant.

"They live on still," she said with a smirk. "Without knowledge of their divine origins or the destiny they were born to."

My entire body went cold. If this were true, I could see why Lucy had chosen this story. I could also see why Ware hadn't wanted to tell me.

"Oh, shit," said Brooklyn. She pointed at one of the monitors I was supposed to be, well, monitoring.

A dark shadow had coalesced in the basement. It had a human form, but its edges were indistinct, as if it were made from smoke.

"Castro!" I shouted. "Basement. Now!"

"What?"

"Shadow person in the basement," yelled Brooklyn. "So get down there right now!"

"Jesus," muttered Andre. "Castro, where's the camera?"

"Got it," said Castro. I heard him dash through the kitchen and rush down the steps.

Brooklyn turned away from the monitors and went into the living room. "Come on, sleepy head," I heard her say to her cousin. "Get downstairs. Castro could use backup."

I stayed with the monitors, though I wanted to be far away from them, and the basement, and the smirking angel sitting across the table from me. Lucy sipped her wine and kept her green eyes focused on me.

I wanted to slap her into next week so badly. Instead, I watched the monitors, where Castro and Andre were now shown wandering the basement, taking pictures.

The shadow person was gone.

6

Castro apparently hadn't really expected to see anything with the unaided eye, as on the video I saw him begin taking photos as soon as he hit the basement, carefully taking photos of every corner of the basement. His demeanor was fairly calm, though in his face, I could see his was somewhat excited. He was thorough.

Andre wasn't nearly as organized. He was more like a terrier, dashing around, looking in corners, turning on as many lights as he could find. Even through the video feed, it was annoying.

"What is he doing?" asked Brooklyn. "Trying to scare it off?"

"He's just excited," I said. "Must be one of those descendants of Gilgamesh Lucy was going on about."

Lucy smiled and winked at me.

"That was just a story," said Brooklyn. "A weird one, but nothing unusual. Lots of cultures have stories about divine beings having children with humans."

I hadn't really thought much about it, but I dimly recalled that Greek heroes like Hercules and Perseus were supposed to be children of Zeus. "Don't they usually end up having a god father and a human mother?"

"Not always," said Brooklyn. "But yeah, that's usually the way it is."

"Maybe all those stories have some grain of truth tied up in them," said Lucy. "Or not. It was just a story. Your basement specter is much more interesting."

"It's gone," I said.

"Is it?"

I looked back at the monitor. All I saw was Andre frantically searching the basement and Castro taking pictures.

"Yeah, it is," I said.

Lucy sighed and asked again, with asperity, "*Is it?*"

I looked up. The shadow person was standing behind Brooklyn, blocking my view of the living room. It was around seven feet tall and wispy. Toward its core, it was deepest black, fading to something like black smoke at what passed for its edges. My heart skipped a beat and my breath caught in my throat.

"Oh."

"What?" asked Brooklyn.

I just kept my eyes on the figure and nodded in that direction. Brooklyn turned around slowly.

"Oh, shit," she said in a low voice. She half-rose from her chair, but then apparently decided there was no point in fleeing, and sat back down. "Teryl, do you have a recorder nearby? We should ask it some questions."

"Ah...I guess so." I pulled out my phone and opened up the camera app. I switched it to video and hit record.

"Okay, go," I said.

"Who are you?" Brooklyn asked. "You can tell us. We're not here to hurt you."

She waited a few seconds before continuing. "Earlier, someone requested our help. Was that you? If not, do you know who it was?"

I took my eyes off the damn shadow figure long enough to check the monitors. Castro had apparently taken as many pictures as he felt were necessary and was headed toward the stairs. Andre followed. He was gesturing as if arguing some point.

Lucy shifted in her seat and the shadow person suddenly appeared to become aware of her. It jerked away from her and vanished. My heart started beating again.

"Wow," said Brooklyn. "A real shadow person." She turned toward me, shaking. Her eyes were wide as if she were shaking in fear, but she was beaming as well. Afraid and excited? Interesting combination. Now that the shadow person was gone, I was gravitating toward just wanting to leave. Ware clearly had some kind of agenda here, and I didn't know what it was. Was I supposed to fight something? Prove myself somehow? Become some kind of ghost hunter that could work with Lucy in the future to do Ware's bidding? Or was it just a test to see if I were going to freak out?

Did I care? One the one hand, no, I did not. I didn't want to be drawn into whatever kind of war Lucy had been warning me about. It was apparently over an old grudge that was none of my business, and that I had no stake in.

On the other hand, I didn't think that I was going to be given a choice except to participate, and having as much information as possible was probably a good idea. My life might actually depend on it, as ridiculous and frightening as that idea might be.

"Yeah, a real shadow person," I said as enthusiastically as I could manage. I don't think I managed it too well; Castro would have known I was faking the interest, but Brooklyn didn't know me that well.

"What did we get? Play back the recording!" she said as Castro and Andre came into the dining room.

"Didn't see anything," Castro reported. "But you probably already noticed that in the monitor."

"That's because it was here," said Brooklyn. She frantically gestured toward my phone. "We should have gotten video of it, maybe audio, too. Play it, Teryl!"

I slid the phone toward the center of the table and played the file. The image clearly showed the shadow person behind Brooklyn. In the recording, she asked, *Who are you?*

I turned the volume up as high as it would go but didn't hear any response until she asked if it knew who had asked for help. There was a faint hiss that might have been *yes.*

No one else seemed to have heard that, though.

"At least you got video of it," said Andre. "I don't want to go back to sleep now. I want to keep an eye on the house. This is exciting!"

"I'm ready to turn in," I said. "The monitors are all yours."

"I'm going to stay up, too," said Castro. "I'll start going through the photos I took downstairs. Maybe there will be something in one of them, even if the shadow person was up here at the time."

"No one said there could only be one," said Andre.

"True," said Castro. "Or there could be a shadow person and something else. We don't know what kind of beings are out there...or in here with us."

"I don't believe anyone does," said Lucy. "As it's a nice night, I'll just head out onto the deck and finish the wine. If anything happens, give a shout and I'll come back inside."

"Okay," said Andre absently.

Castro looked at me with a questioning expression. He knew the truth about the Forlorn, and knew Lucy was one of them, but obviously couldn't ask anything too obvious in front of Brooklyn and Andre.

I shrugged. I had no idea if Lucy and Ware's plan required her to be outside, or if she just didn't want to spend any more time in the house around four humans.

I stood up and Andre took my chair. "Night," I said.

Castro looked up at me with that brilliant smile that had been one of the first things I'd noticed about him in the store where we'd first met. I bent down to kiss him on the lips.

"Hey, get a room," said Andre.

"Actually, I have an entire apartment I could be sleeping in right now," I said. "But instead, I'm here with you."

Andre laughed and waved me away. "See you in a bit. Sleep well."

Brooklyn just gave me a tired smile. "I'm staying up," she said.

"Fine with me."

I went back to the living room and climbed into Castro's sleeping bag. My gaze flicked around the room as I searched for the shadow person, but I saw nothing but the regular furniture and the light streaming from the dining room into the foyer.

I closed my eyes and hoped I'd be able to get to sleep, but the floor was harder than my bed at home, and I heard Castro and Andre chatting in the other room. Occasionally, the house gave up a random creak which sounded enough like the kind of noises I had in my apartment that I did not find them alarming. Buildings make noises; that was the way of things. This might be a haunted house, but that didn't mean it didn't make ordinary sounds, too.

Eventually, I must have fallen asleep, because the next thing I knew, I was opening my eyes to a dark house. I rubbed my eyes and realized the dining room was now dark and I heard nothing from any of the others. I looked over at Andre's sleeping bag and it was lumpy as if someone were in it. I couldn't tell who, though.

Someone seemed to be on the couch. Perhaps the fourth person was in the dining room with the monitors but had the overhead light off. I settled back down and closed my eyes.

The quiet was so thick, I wondered what it was that had awakened me. Was it too much to ask for more than a couple of hours of uninterrupted sleep?

Maybe on a ghost hunt, that was too much to ask. At least I could try to get back to sleep and hope the next time I opened my eyes, it would be morning.

A footfall. Then another. I opened my eyes. Without moving my head, I glanced around. Lucy was coming across the room, headed for the stairs to the second floor.

As she moved, she stepped carefully and slowly, clearly not wanting to wake up the humans. I waited until she got up the steps before sliding out of the sleeping bag. I thought it was time to figure out why she was really here.

7

I tried to be as quiet as possible, but of course, Lucy had supernaturally good hearing. She was waiting for me at the top of the stairs. She raised an eyebrow.

I crossed my arms and waited to see if she would explain, or at least continue to her destination. After a few moments, she rolled her eyes and turned back to the master bedroom. She went straight to the en suite.

I closed the bedroom door behind us so we could talk without waking anyone else. "What are you doing? Is this something to do with Ware?"

She shrugged. "Yes and no. Ware likes to ask for favors without always being truthful about why he wants them. So, yes, he asked me to come. But I don't know if I'll be doing exactly what he wants. I need to know more first."

That seemed reasonable. Ware was pretty tight-lipped. He hadn't even wanted me to know what little I did, but had only agreed that I be told a bare minimum when he felt he had no other choice.

"So what are you looking for?"

She glanced at the ceiling, finally opening the walk-in closet door and pointing up. "That."

I looked in, but the closet was pitch black. "I just have human eyesight, you know," I said.

She looked a little startled. "Oh."

"And that's a surprise because?"

She gave me a measuring stare. "You understand the Forlorn, like me and Ware, are all different, right?"

"Fish is telepathic when not drunk, yes," I said, "and Oya can possess people. Ware can give people some kind of power through the use of his real name." I raised my right hand, where a pinkish scar on my palm spelled out Ware's name in his native script. To me, it looked like a circle crossed with a few squiggly lines. "I don't know what you can do, though."

"Water is my element," she said. "I could drag you under the surface of a pond and you wouldn't need to breathe as long as I had my hands on you. I've had a lot of names over the centuries. Jenny Greenteeth is the one I like best."

"Then why don't you go by Jenny rather than Lucy?" I asked.

She stifled a laugh. "Good question." She paused. "Guess I just like Lucy, at least for now."

"And what does that have to do with me?" I'd asked her about me, and she'd immediately deflected to talk about her own kind.

"The Lost have their own powers," she said.

I gritted my teeth. I had been told several times now that I was *Lost*. Like, with a capital L. It meant I was someone special. If Lucy's fanciful story from the kitchen were at least somewhat true, it meant I was descended from Gilgamesh and an angel somehow. I decided to push that utterly insane idea aside and focus on what was in front of me.

I pointed at the closet. "Okay, so, Jenny Greenteeth, what's in the closet my poor mortal eyes can't see?"

"Access to the attic," she said.

"I don't think these homes have attics."

"Crawlspace? Do you like that better? There's space between the ceiling and the roofline. Pick a word for it; I don't care."

I didn't care, either. Why not use her word? "What do you expect to find in this attic?"

"The thing Ware wants."

My turn to say "oh" with no follow-up.

She felt around inside the closet until she found a light switch, which she flicked on. The sudden burst of light out of the closet blinded me and I blinked and turned my head.

By the time my eyes had adjusted, Lucy had lowered a kind of trap door and had lowered a ladder. Having lived in a succession of cheap apartments for my entire life, I'd never seen such a thing in person. But I did recall seeing something similar in some TV shows.

"Coming up?" she asked as she began climbing the ladder.

The dark hole in the ceiling of the closet was hardly inviting. "I don't have a flashlight," I said. "And now my eyes are used to the light. What do you suppose I'll see if I go up there?"

Lucy poked her head into the attic space and she scanned the area. "I'd tell you you'd see some garbage, a pile of what appears to be Christmas lights, a couple of pieces of cheap framed art, a chair, and a small box, like the kind little girls put their costume jewelry in."

"In other words, junk."

"That would be it," she said. "Unless there's something hiding under the Christmas lights."

"So what is Ware interested in?"

"The box?" she asked. "It's small and portable. I doubt Christmas lights fit the bill. Or the tacky art from some yard sale or other."

"You don't know? He didn't tell you what to look for?"

"I believe he feels it should be obvious."

That seemed like Ware all over.

"What are all these items that interest him?" I asked.

"Stuff from an ancient time," said Lucy. "Not all of our kind can utilize their power, though."

"Because you're all different."

"Something like that."

Lucy continued climbing into the attic. "Hang on. I'm going to grab the box."

She disappeared into the blackness. I heard her rustling around, but within seconds she was back. Her white arm came down through the opening, holding a small box, the kind that was a music box, too. I'd never owned one, but I'd seen them before. You wound up the spring, opened the box, and a ballerina spun around in front of a mirror that was affixed to the inside of the lid.

"Take it," said Lucy. "It'll be hard for me to climb down the ladder with only one hand."

I reached up and took the box from her, then backed out of the closet and waited for her to join me.

The box, surely, wasn't what Ware wanted. I shook it gently and heard something rolling around inside.

"So, what's inside?" asked Lucy as she backed down the ladder.

The last time I'd seen a box with a magic object inside of it, bad things had happened as long as the box had been open. I wasn't opening this one right now, not for anything.

"You'll have to look for yourself," I said.

"No guts, no glory," said Lucy. "Isn't that what humans say?"

"Humans say lots of stupid shit," I said. I handed the box back to her.

Lucy shrugged. She opened the box. Inside was a large red marble, a penny, two hair clips, and a pencil stub whose eraser was completely worn down to nothing.

"Exciting," I said, trying to disguise both my alarm that she'd just opened something that could be holding a terrifically powerful magical item, and my disappointment at what was actually contained inside.

"One never knows," she said. "I'll have to take it to Ware and let him sort it out."

"Better you than me," I said. "Does this mean you're now officially off the ghost hunt?"

"I suppose, yes, officially," she said, as she placed the box in the cross body bag she still had strapped around her chest. "But I'm finding the four of you amusing to watch, so I think I'll stay."

"Glad we could amuse you," I said. "I'm going back to sleep."

Lucy pushed the ladder back up and then used a stick I hadn't previously noticed to lift the trap door back up into place.

"You do that," she said. "I think there's another bottle of white in the kitchen. Might as well finish that before I start in on the reds."

Angels. They all seemed to be ridiculously addicted to alcohol. Maybe it wasn't just Fish who found it dulled supernaturally-sharp senses to a more comfortable background annoyance. I couldn't imagine being able to read thoughts, or hear people blocks away, or whatever, and then have to cope with that every hour of every day for...well, forever.

At least our civilization could offer them some respite from the overwhelming nature of their senses and the kind of sensitivity they had to live with all the time. Whether it was funny or tragic that alcohol was the thing that could give them a moment's peace escaped me.

I turned away and opened the door to the corridor and Lucy turned off the closet light. The darkness I was plunged into was absolute enough that, for now, I was blind. I felt along the wall toward the stairs and made my way carefully down them. I was special, after all, and couldn't afford to be sidelined in the upcoming war because I was stupid and had fallen down some stairs, right?

I sighed and decided I didn't want to sleep, after all. I went to the dining room to sit with the monitors. Brooklyn was still there, but she had fallen asleep in her chair. I took the chair opposite had and watched the monitors, which all showed absolutely nothing unusual.

The time stamp on the monitors read 4:08. I kept my eyes on it and eventually it moved to 4:09. I rested my chin on my hand and wished I felt tired enough to go back to the sleeping bag.

In the kitchen, Lucy rustled around, and I heard the sound of a popping cork. I almost called out to her to pour me a glass, but decided against it.

On the monitor, something moved in the basement. Not the shadow person, something much smaller. Probably a mouse.

I picked up a pen and jotted a note down on the notepad that sat on the table. I saw that Andre had previously written,

2:01 *Shadow moves across kitchen*

2:45 *Orbs circling around master bedroom*

3:04 *Flicker of light in kitchen. Probably headlights of car*

My note of 4:09 *shadow in basement, probably mouse* looked just as unimpressive as it sounded.

The monitor time stamp moved to 4:10. Boredom was setting in. I sighed and waited for...something. I had no idea what, but I was betting the house wasn't finished with us yet.

8

Brooklyn stirred around five a.m. She yawned and glanced around, saw me, and smiled. "Guess I didn't stay up all night, after all."

"Guess not. You haven't missed much." I showed her the log.

She nodded. "I saw Andre's notes. So there's just your single note at, um, 4:09. Nothing since then, I guess."

"Nope." I glanced at the darkness outside. "Shouldn't the sun be coming up?"

"At five? No, more like seven," she said. "It's October. Soon we'll fall back and dawn will be more like six again."

I closed my eyes, suddenly exhausted, even if I didn't feel sleepy. Just the thought of coping with the semi-annual time change made me tired. I hated it, both in the spring and fall. I always felt poorly rested and stressed for a full week after. Why can't we just be on daylight saving time all year?

"Shouldn't the guys have been taking the rest of the night shift?" I asked.

Brooklyn laughed softly. "Andre was so tired, he fell asleep at the table. I led him to the couch and he just crashed on it. Castro only made it maybe ten more minutes, and then he just went to the other sleeping bag and turned in without a word."

I glanced at the monitors, but all seemed calm. "So, you're Andre's cousin? And you're living with him? He usually doesn't have anywhere to stay himself."

Brooklyn nodded. "Yeah. We actually agreed to go in on an apartment together, but then, while I was out of town, he found a cheaper one and signed the lease himself. So I'm technically living in his apartment, but we're splitting the expenses. I've heard a lot about Castro, and about you, too. I know you're some of the friends that he crashes with in between apartments and girlfriends."

"Yeah, but not for a few months now. I hadn't heard about you, though. Andre doesn't talk much about his family."

Brooklyn looked sad. "Yeah, well, his mom died a long time ago, and his dad wasn't around much. He hung out with me, my siblings, and my parents mostly. We tried to make him feel welcome, but it was hard. He missed his mom and his dad didn't always keep a working phone or email address, so he was in and out of Andre's life. That's my uncle, my mom's brother. I can remember her being so mad at Uncle Trent when Andre's birthday would come and go without a word from him. She'd go all out to make Andre feel special, but you can't make up for some things."

"No, I guess you can't," I said.

"Honestly, I swear I don't understand how my mom and Uncle Trent came from the same parents. They are *nothing* alike. My mom would give her last penny to someone who needed it more, and she practically doted on every friend I ever had over to the house. If she knew they had problems, then even more. Like, one year she found out my friend Megan hadn't had new shoes for ages because her parents couldn't afford it, and then Megan comes to school one day all happy because she won some kind of contest and got new shoes. I know it was my mom orchestrating something so Megan and her family didn't have to feel like they were taking charity. And then here's her brother, off doing who-knows-what, and can't even be bothered to call his kid on his birthday."

"Your mom sounds great," I said.

"Most of the time," she said with a smile. "How about yours?"

"Oh, mine's a jerk," I said. "I don't talk to her much anymore. Castro's parents are dead. He grew up in the foster system."

I never embellished the bare facts of my life or Castro's. That usually put people off enough that they stopped asking questions.

Brooklyn wasn't most people. "That's sad," she said. "Especially for you. I mean, Castro knows he can't talk to his parents, but you could talk to your mom."

"There's no point," I said. "We've said all we need to say."

Maybe *that* would get her to change the topic.

I'd never know, because that was when Lucy popped into the dining room from the kitchen. She now had a glass of red wine in her hand, so she must have finished that other bottle of white.

"I suggest you get your intrepid ghost hunting friends up and go downstairs. Something's happening."

I checked the monitors, but all remained the same.

"I don't care if it shows up on your screens," she said. "I can just feel it. And I'm the expert, right?"

"Okay," said Brooklyn. She got up and left the dining room.

"You're going to need some things," said Lucy. "Salt, quartz, sidewalk chalk, cotton bag with a drawstring. Did anyone bring those things?"

"What?" I asked stupidly. Ware hadn't said anything about supplies.

Lucy rolled her eyes. "I figured. I already called Fish. He's dropping off the stuff in a few minutes."

"Fish?" I didn't think Fish had a car, and this neighborhood was too far for him to walk from downtown in a few minutes.

"Ware will lend him a car, and Fish *can* drive, even if he hates doing it. So keep an eye out for him."

Brooklyn came back in the room. "Did I hear you say we need things like salt?"

I shrugged, answering the question I saw in her eyes. "Lucy said it. I don't know what we need the stuff for. Are we casting some kind of spell to protect us or something?"

Lucy said casually, "No. You're going to make a prison. You want to catch what's downstairs and get it out of the house."

"I do? I mean, we do?"

Brooklyn looked at Lucy. "You can *catch* ghosts? I thought you had to exorcise them or get them to go to the light or something."

"Aren't you supposed to be the sensitive one?" Lucy asked sarcastically.

"I can sense spirits, or at least, strange energies," said Brooklyn. "But I've never *caught* anything. I've been to haunted places where people used sage to cleanse the location and to encourage spirits to move on. I've never been to an actual exorcism, though. That's too scary. I don't want to meet a demon."

Lucy didn't say anything to that, but her eye roll said it all. I was just glad Brooklyn was now looking down at her own hands and didn't see that. Lucy didn't have to be so smug about knowing more than Brooklyn. She was a freaking immortal celestial being, more than likely one of the beings that was the source of the legends of angels and demons, and Brooklyn was a twenty-something human being who didn't have any supernatural powers. The best she could do, assuming she actually had some special sense about ghosts, was to be able to pick out the energy of dead people before they faded away.

It wasn't exactly fair to hold Brooklyn responsible for not knowing what was really going on. Hell, I barely knew what was going on, and didn't really want to know more.

I just wasn't going to be given a choice.

Castro and Andre came into the room.

"Downstairs?" asked Castro. His hair, even though it was quite short, now stuck out from his head at every angle. His eyes were red-rimmed, but his demeanor was that of someone interested and engaged. So losing some sleep had only made him tired. It hadn't diminished his enthusiasm.

"We need supplies, apparently," I said drily. "Fish is on his way with the stuff we need."

Castro and Andre looked to Lucy as she nodded at my response.

"Supplies?" asked Castro. "Why didn't we know about that?"

"Because Ware couldn't be bothered to inform Teryl before she came," said Lucy. "But I've got it covered. When Fish gets here, I'm going to need you to draw this on the basement floor." She took a pen and a piece of notebook paper and scribbled a bizarre design that vaguely looked like a pentagram, but had additional shapes and crisscross lines on it.

It reminded me of the brand on my hand. This had to be Lucy's real name, the one in her own language.

"That's what the sidewalk chalk is for," she said. "Then, once things start happening, make a circle of salt outside the design to seal the ghost and the sign inside the salt. When you're ready to grab the thing, put one of the quartz crystals in the bag, and the others here." She marked five spots on the design.

"And then we just grab it and shove it in the bag?" asked Andre with a frown. "That doesn't seem right. They never do that on the shows I watch."

"Who's the expert here?" asked Lucy. "Not those jerks on the TV who scare themselves by filming in the dark and jumping at every creak. What do they know? They wave their sage around and claim they've cleansed something. More than likely, there was never anything there to begin with. Hauntings are exceedingly rare. Humans fooling themselves into believing there's a haunting is far more common."

"Okay," said Castro, cutting off Andre, who seemed about to say something. "You're the expert. Assuming this works, and we catch the thing, then what?"

"Then you give it to me," said Lucy. "And I will take it away and send it onward. There's no need for you to be involved with that."

I didn't like the way she said that. I'd seen Oya treat a human soul like garbage, and Ware had one roaming his office like some kind of neglected pet. If the basement of this house truly contained a soul, a *scrap*, as Lucy said, she wouldn't be gently ushering it on to the next world. She'd be turning it over to Ware, who would use whatever power it held for some purpose of his own.

Lucy looked at me and gave me a strange grin. She knew this thing in the basement was going to a far different fate than she let on.

But was it a better fate, or a worse one, than what it would experience trapped in this house? That I had no answer to.

9

The sun was touching the horizon by the time Fish finally got to the house. His lanky figure climbed out of the car and he went around back to lift the hatch and grab a sack.

As usual, his clothes hung on him and his shoes looked as though they were being held together with good thoughts alone; it was as if their structural integrity were just waiting to give way at the worst moment.

Fish's hangdog expression and his crazy spiked hair were the same as always. The dawn sun glinted off the red highlights that mingled with the dark brown.

Lucy opened the front door before he could ring the bell. She opened the door wide and Fish strolled in.

"Hey," he said to me. He nodded to Castro.

"Andre," I said, nodding toward him. "Brooklyn. This is Fish. He's a regular at the bar where I work."

Brooklyn looked troubled by this. Maybe she had some kind of bias against barflies? She hadn't looked twice at Lucy drinking at least four bottles of wine without consuming a bite of food, but she frowned at hearing Fish was a regular at the Angels' Share?

Lucy dumped the contents of the bag out on the dining room table. She grabbed one of the packages of sidewalk chalk—for some reason, Fish had brought six of those—and ripped it open. "Color doesn't matter," she said as she handed the pink chalk to Castro. "Take the drawing I made and go down and draw it on the floor. Just make sure you leave enough space to make the salt circle around it later."

"So, why aren't you making it?" asked Brooklyn. Her troubled look had not diminished.

"Because experts get to give the orders, not do the peon shit," she said lightly.

Fish made a sour face. I was going to guess he didn't like how rude Lucy was being, but didn't feel strong enough to directly confront her. It had become clear that Fish occupied some nebulous social position among his peers. Yes, he was Forlorn, an angel-type being, one of their own. But he was also rather hapless and pitiful, worse than some humans, if the rolled eyes, sighs, and verbal slights were any indication.

I couldn't imagine being one of these things that had belonged to a star-faring race for millions of years, and who were now trapped on one planet, wingless, almost powerless when compared to their former selves. Shadows, almost, when compared to their earlier lives. Fish clearly longed to be gone from here, to once again be able to explore the universe, propelling himself from star to star, or maybe even reality to reality, on willpower and wings.

To be reduced from that to *barfly* was definitely a far way to fall. Fish clearly grieved for his former life. Ware, Lucy, and the others had seemed to make some kind of peace with it. I got the feeling some of them, like Ware, might actually prefer their life on earth over their life before. My sense was that, in their previous lives, they rarely encountered one another, and spent much of their eternal lives utterly alone. Sure, the universe was beautiful and splendid and awe-inspiring, but it was difficult to appreciate it when you were incomprehensibly lonely.

At least, that's what I had managed to piece together from the little digs and slips Ware and his fellows made. I could have pieced those things together incorrectly.

"Fine," said Castro. He grabbed the piece of paper that contained Lucy's scribble and headed toward the basement. Andre picked up a camera and followed.

I watched the monitors as Castro and Andre made their way down the stairs. Castro looked at the floor, then the drawing. He decided where to start drawing and began making the symbol on the concrete floor.

The more he drew, the darker the basement got, or at least the dimmer the feed got on the monitor. "What's up with that?" I asked, pointing at the dimming screen.

Lucy said nothing, nor did Fish. Brooklyn gave them both a wary glance. Had she somehow figured out Fish was more than an ordinary guy, and that Lucy was like him? Or was it just their attitudes that were getting to her?

Fish had entered the dining room but stood as far as possible from Brooklyn. Lucy had stopped paying attention to anything except the materials on the table. She carefully picked up, inspected, and put down each crystal. After she had done this several times, I realized she was sorting them into piles.

"Are they in trouble?" asked Brooklyn to no one in particular. "Should we go down there to help?"

"We'll only be in the way," said Lucy absently. "Let them finish. The real fight won't start until we get the crystals down there." She pointed at one of her piles. The crystals in each looked identical to me, but clearly they weren't to Lucy. "These crystals are good enough to use. The rest are garbage."

"They were what I could find," said Fish defensively.

"I know," she said without rancor. "And they might do for a different situation. But for this thing in the basement today, we need *these* crystals."

"They all look the same," said Brooklyn.

"But they're not," said Lucy. "I can tell the difference. I'm the expert, remember?"

There was no getting around the sarcasm in her voice. Brooklyn didn't care for it. She crossed her arms and took a slight step back from Lucy. Lucy didn't notice, or at least appeared not to.

By now, it was difficult to see what Castro was doing. Andre only appeared in the frame occasionally; he was taking pictures of the basement. He was also being careful not to step on the design Castro was making. Lucy nodded as she watched.

"Once they're finished with that, I'll take the crystals down. The rest of you each grab a bag of salt and come down once I have the first crystal in place. At that point, we don't stop. You do as I say, and we finish, or it'll be like we never started."

10

I watched as Castro finished the design in chalk on the floor. He put the chalk down and looked at the camera.

"Time to go," said Lucy. She picked up the crystals she had chosen as being the best for this situation. "Remember to take a bag of salt each."

We each grabbed a sandwich bag that had already been filled with salt. Even Fish grabbed one. I looked at him, surprised. I would have thought he would have delivered the materials, and then retreated to the Angels' Share to begin his daily rounds of alcohol.

He shrugged. "Ware said if I stayed to help, I drink free later tonight. Maybe tomorrow, too."

Huh. My boss was certainly interested in whatever was in this house. Recruiting me, Lucy, and now Fish.

What was in the basement?

Lucy led the way. I followed with Fish just behind me. Brooklyn took up the rear. I wondered if she were regretting coming, or if she wanted to be as far from Lucy as possible.

Once we got to the basement, Lucy pointed to where she wanted us to stand. She handed bags of salt to Castro and Andre. "I'm going to place the crystals now," she said. "It's important for the four...five...of you," she shot a sideways glance at Fish, "to stay where you are, no matter what happens. The spirit will try to escape, but it won't be able to if this goes right."

"And if it doesn't?" I asked.

"Then we make sure it's still in the house and start over. We'll have to wait a couple of hours for the power from the first try to dissipate. That'll be enough time to get something to eat, take a break, and reorganize."

"Let's just make sure it works the first time," said Brooklyn. "I don't know if I can do this twice."

"You getting something?" asked Andre.

She glanced around nervously. "It's definitely down here," she said. "I can feel the heaviness in the air. Can't you?"

"No," I said.

Castro and Andre both shook their heads. Fish behaved as if he hadn't heard the question.

"It's frightened, I think," said Brooklyn. "Maybe a little angry at being disturbed. Mostly I feel its fear."

"They're all afraid, dear," said Lucy. "They're trapped here and that frightens them. We help them by removing them from this plane of existence."

I bit my lip and wondered how truthful the *we help them* part was. I wasn't going to put much faith in that statement. I think it was more *we do whatever we want with them.*

I think whatever was in the basement had a pretty good reason to be afraid. It had been targeted by Ware and he'd sent Lucy to collect it. But collect it for what?

Lucy kissed the first crystal and placed it in the very center of the design while she faced Brooklyn. The lights flickered. Brooklyn looked around anxiously but a flickering light wasn't going to be enough to startle me into running after what I'd seen over the past month.

Lucy closed her eyes, took out a second crystal and held it to her forehead, then opened her eyes, stepped forward and put the crystal down in front of Castro.

A horrible keening began coming from the back corner of the basement. The sound was like fingernails on a chalkboard; it was impossible not to recoil from it. The sound grated against eardrums and seemed to scrape down each nerve to the very ends of my toes.

Lucy took a third crystal, moved in front of Andre and placed the thing at his feet, on a spot where five of the sidewalk chalk lines came together.

The keening changed in tone and now a shadow appeared in the corner. It appeared to be writhing in agony and dropped to its insubstantial knees.

I assume Lucy saw it, but she gave no indication. Instead, she held a fourth crystal. This one she held up four times. I was disoriented in the basement, but I assumed she was holding it out to the four cardinal directions. Then she touched it to each shoulder and put it down in front of Fish, who appeared somewhat anxious but not as anxious as the rest of us. Of course, he was an eternal deathless being, too. Whatever this thing was, it couldn't harm him. It was the four humans in the basement who were actually risking harm.

I had to assume harm was possible or there'd be no point in the salt, right? I thought salt was for protection or something like that.

Besides, people who'd moved out of the house had reported being shoved or punched. So the spirit or spirits here could certainly do *some* harm, even if it was pretty lame stuff in the grand scheme of things.

Lucy had a fifth crystal in her hands now. She held it over her head and began chanting in some guttural language. The shadow, which at this point had puddled onto the floor as if no longer able to hold on to a humanoid shape, started slithering into the chalk shape, as if it were a snake of dark smoke or fog.

As soon as the thing was completely inside the design, Lucy slammed the fifth crystal down in front of me and shouted something incomprehensible.

The snake-thing screamed and reformed into a human shape, but then slowly collapsed in on itself. It spread out toward the edges of the shape.

"Get the salt down," said Lucy. "Make an unbroken circle. Start in front of yourself and work right until you get to the next person's part of the circle. Quickly, now."

I opened the baggie and pulled out a handful of salt. I started sprinkling at my feet and moved to my right, toward Andre, who was doing exactly what I was. I made it about halfway to Andre's salt line before having to draw out a second handful.

The salt circle was completed in just a few seconds, leaving us on the outside, and Lucy and the thing inside.

Lucy opened the empty cloth bag and approached the thing. It screamed again and recoiled, but the moment it hit the ring of salt, a bright purple flash flared out from the point of contact, temporarily blinding me with its intensity.

When I could see again, I saw that Brooklyn had fallen to her knees, hands over her ears, eyes screwed shut. She screamed, "Stop it! Stop it!" I didn't know if she were screaming at the shadow thing or Lucy, but it didn't matter. Whatever was happening inside the salt circle wasn't anything we could influence.

I glanced at Fish, but he seemed impatient, not frightened. Perhaps he'd seen rituals like this before, and this wasn't a particularly impressive one.

Lucy held out the bag, shouted something, and slammed the bag down over the shadow. She wrestled with it for a few moments, but before I knew it, she had the whole thing in the sack and she tied the sack shut.

Whatever was inside was now still. The bag was clearly full, but the thing wasn't struggling at this point.

Lucy smiled widely. "That's done it."

Andre and Castro looked shell-shocked, maybe from the horrific screaming of the last minute or two. Brooklyn remained on her knees, sobbing softly.

Fish had perked up a little. I assumed he was now free to go back to the bar and drink his fill, on the house. That should be enough to motivate him to leave quickly.

"So," I said. "Is this hunt now over? Do we just go home?"

"That's up to you," said Lucy, "but I think there's a second thing in this house, and it will put up a worse fight than this poor creature. Crystals and salt won't be enough to trap it."

"No," said Brooklyn. "You tortured that thing. It was in pain, and you hurt it more."

Lucy snorted. "It's like a cat that doesn't want to go in the carrier because it knows it's going to the vet. It doesn't understand the vet is there to help."

"And what you're doing helps?" asked Andre. "Really? Because that thing seemed awfully disturbed by what just happened."

"I can now take it somewhere to release it. You could say, into its own element? Back into the wild? I don't know of a great way to describe it. I'm simply saying it was trapped here, and now it can go somewhere else and have the freedom it deserves."

Fish dropped his baggie onto the floor, where it spread its remaining salt on the floor at his feet. "Well, wherever you take it, I guess it's good riddance. I'm out of here and ready for a few shots of whiskey."

"What'll it be tonight?" I asked. "Jeff is on shift this evening, right?"

"Jeff will be serving me Four Roses small batch," said Fish, "and if I get tired of that, I'll just move on to Buffalo Trace."

"A bourbon night," I said. "You should go for the more expensive stuff if Ware's giving you an open tab."

"I dare not presume," said Fish. He waved and headed toward the steps.

Brooklyn had stopped crying and had watched this byplay with some interest. I wondered if that were why Fish had engaged with me; he'd seen that Brooklyn was now more calm and not sobbing anymore. That could be his second good deed of the day, if you counted for helping trap a human soul in a bag a good deed.

That would presume that Fish felt some compassion for Brooklyn and for how upset she'd been, and I wasn't sure I could go that far. Fish seemed a pathetic sort, but not necessarily someone sympathetic to the griefs and issues of the humans around him. Of course, I could be wrong. It wasn't like I really knew the guy all that well. Or wanted to.

"Time for a break," said Lucy as she swept the salt around the floor with her foot, breaking the circle. I looked at her crystals, but they had crumbled into shiny piles of sand.

"So what else is in the house?" asked Castro. He seemed particularly interested. Neither Brooklyn or Andre appeared as if they really wanted an answer to that question. Brooklyn headed for the steps right behind Fish, and Andre did the same after shaking his head at Castro.

Lucy waited until the others were up the stairs. "The thing we really need to catch," she said. "Somewhere in this house is something very valuable: the soul of an individual who was Lost."

"Lost?" asked Castro. "Like Teryl?"

"Like Teryl," said Lucy. "The Lost are powerful in life, and can be even more powerful in death. This one is a little bastard that's escaped Ware before. This time, I intend to catch it and get it in the damn bag."

"Let me guess," I said, my mouth dry with fear. "I think I know what we're looking for. It's a *scrap*."

Lucy just smiled and nodded.

11

"Scrap?" asked Castro.

"That papery thing I said I saw in Ware's office," I said.

Lucy clutched her bag full of shadow creature. "Things like *this* are made of human spirits from ordinary people. They're generally not just one person, but more like an amalgamation of ten, twenty, even more. They usually last a few days, but if conditions are right, and there are enough new spirits added over time, they can last for years. That's really rare, though. This one's probably one in a million. But the Lost? They can become little bastards like that ankle biter Ware's got right away."

"So scraps are dead humans who were Lost," said Castro slowly, "while these shadow things are conglomerations of dead people. But most dead people just fade away? There's no afterlife?"

Lucy shrugged. "Not as far as any of us knows. Humans die and whatever energy signature they have that remains degrades quickly and simply evaporates. A few minutes at the very least. A few days at most."

"Except for the ones that clump together," said Castro. "How and why do they do that?"

Lucy looked down at her armful of lump bag. "No one really knows. Maybe there are actual energy vortices like the ones that are supposedly around Sedona, or maybe ley lines are real. Maybe the paranormal investigators are right and people who have unfinished business don't fade away as quickly as everyone else. In any case, under some conditions no one's entirely figured out, human energy signatures—call them souls—can join up. Like beads of liquid mercury, sort of. As the older ones fade out, new ones can join, which can make the haunting last longer than a couple of days."

"But the individual inside the conglomeration fade out quickly. It's only that new ones keep joining up that keeps the thing going," I said.

"That's what it seems like. I'm not going to swear that's what's going on all the time, because no one really knows, but that does seem to cover it, more or less."

"And what does Ware want with them?"

Lucy laughed. "Now that's none of my business to tell. You'll have to ask Ware."

"You know he won't say."

She turned away and headed up the stairs. "That's your problem. Mine is now trying to figure out where that scrap it, and setting a trap for it."

As she went up the stairs, Castro turned to me and gestured toward the upstairs. "What do we tell Andre and Brooklyn? They think we've solved the problem, and Lucy wants to catch something even more dangerous that she clearly doesn't want to tell them about."

I shrugged. "I guess we tell them we're supposed to stay here all weekend, and we want to see if we can get any more readings, even though we've caught the one thing we saw earlier on the monitors?"

"Maybe we give them some story about vortices?" suggested Castro. "Although first we'd have to figure out what we think those even are."

I tried to remember some obscure fact from one of the shows Castro had watched. "Maybe you fell asleep on this one, but do you remember the ley lines theory? Sounds like it's an idea that Lucy might even buy in to."

Castro nodded. "They're supposed to be energy lines in between sacred sites or something. Of course, it might be a hard sell to say this modern house has somehow, by virtue of some amazing coincidence, been built on a place where ley lines converge."

"Doesn't have to be coincidence," I said. "Maybe the line that connects Stonehenge and some site in the southwest United States passes right through this neighborhood. You don't know."

"We can always go with that," said Castro. He ran both hands through his short hair and yawned. "I could really use a shower and some caffeine. Last night was a long one."

"You're the one who likes the idea of hunting ghosts."

"You're the one plagued by the supernatural," he retorted.

True enough. "Let's get something to eat and then see what Lucy wants us to do to find this scrap."

Castro put a hand on my arm. "Hold on. Do we actually want her to *catch* it? I mean, apparently, *you're* going to be a scrap someday. What would you want someone to do with *your* soul?"

I shuddered. "I can't even think about that this morning. I'm going to go along with this for now, and pick up whatever information I can. I just know that neither Ware nor Lucy probably feels any compunction about injuring, or even destroying, this scrap. They want it caught for their own purposes. So, while I'll cooperate for now, I'm going to keep my eyes and my options open."

Castro nodded. "Sounds good. I've got your back."

I smiled and leaned over to kiss him. "Got yours, too."

We went upstairs. Andre had pulled out two bags of frosted doughnuts, the small round kind with either powdered sugar or chocolate coating. He had also poured several glasses of orange juice. I smelled coffee but didn't see a coffeemaker.

Andre gestured toward the microwave. "Zapping instant coffee into existence right here," he said. "Sorry, no Keurig or percolator around."

"Microwaving is just fine," I said. Honestly, I could live without coffee if I had to, but Castro liked it and clearly Andre wanted some. My assumption was that Lucy would go for another bottle of wine, if there actually were any more. Brooklyn was staring at the microwave with an intensity that made me believe she was also a coffee fiend.

"So, after breakfast, do we pack up and leave?" asked Andre. "I've got a date for dinner."

Brooklyn smiled a bit at that; she'd no doubt been privy to a lot of Andre's discussions of all his latest dating hookups.

"We're staying," said Castro. "You can go if you want. There's only one more night. We'll be leaving tomorrow sometime."

Andre looked undecided. Brooklyn said, "I'm staying, too. At least, when I feel something in this house, you guys take me seriously."

"Good," said Lucy. She stood in the archway between the kitchen and the living room. Sleeping bags lay in a pile behind her. I did not look forward to using one on the floor again. I wondered if I should just take a couch. Why not? Who was going to kick me off of it once I claimed it?

"Why good?" asked Andre.

"Because there's something else in this house, and I need to understand it better."

I took that as code for *this is the thing I really came here for, but I don't think you need to know that.*

Brooklyn seemed to have an idea that Lucy was not revealing what she really meant. Castro already knew. Andre appeared oblivious. Actually, he was more focused on the hot water, which was almost done heating in the microwave.

"How do we find it?" I asked.

"You and Brooklyn need to go through the house, room by room, and where you feel something watching you, well, that's probably it."

"Now that you've said that, I'll probably feel someone watching me in every room," I said under my breath.

Lucy raised a glass of wine to me. "Probably. But it will help if you and Brooklyn take notes in each room and don't let each other know what you feel or what you're writing. Then we'll see if any of your observations line up to a certain place in the house."

"Breakfast first," said Brooklyn. "Though I don't really want to eat those stupid doughnuts. Didn't you get any fruit or bread when you went shopping?"

Andre shrugged. "I never eat fruit for breakfast. Didn't occur to me. There's some cheese and crackers. I could put another pizza in the oven."

"Pizza for breakfast?" Brooklyn seemed insulted by the very idea. Personally, I was fine with the doughnuts since it was only going to be for today. Tomorrow we'd be packing up, and Castro and I could eat a late breakfast at home, or stop to get something on the way that was not doughnuts.

Andre just shrugged again and opened the microwave to pull out the cups of hot water. "I've got those instant packets," he said, nodding toward the end of the counter where little colored foil wrappers lay haphazardly one on top of the other. "I think regular, French vanilla, and hazelnut are the choices."

Everyone made their own coffee, and everyone, including Brooklyn, took some doughnuts. She opted for the powdered sugar ones.

Breakfast was over quickly. I felt a little better with some hot coffee in me and at least a few bites of something that was, if not great, at least edible.

"All right," I said. "I'll start upstairs. Why don't you start on this floor, Brooklyn, and we'll switch. That way we won't give away any clues by being in the same room at the same time."

She nodded. We each got a pad of paper from the dining room and I went up the stairs.

Honestly, the entire house was now creeping me out. Seeing the shadow person, and hearing it scream and writhe around on the floor had put a damper on this little adventure. Now every shadow seemed to hold some menace. Every creak of the floor felt like it came from something following me and not my own feet.

The master suite felt heavier today. I don't know how else to describe it. It was like the light entering the room immediately dimmed upon entry. Sounds were muffled, as if by stepping into this space, I had entered another world. I jotted notes down and quickly went to the other rooms. They all felt off, but not like the master suite.

I went down the stairs. Brooklyn appeared a few moments later and went up. I then wandered the ground floor, but nothing stood out to me. I took a deep breath and headed for the basement.

"It won't be down there," said Lucy placidly. "Since that's where the shadow was hanging out, it's the one place we can be sure the other thing is not."

"They don't like each other or something?" asked Andre.

"More like, one's a predator and one is prey," said Lucy. "They won't have been snuggling up together singing Kumbaya."

That made me shiver. When I died, I could become a scrap, and a scrap was a *predator*? A predator who, what, *ate* human souls?

Tears misted my eyes but I blinked them away. All too well, I remembered meeting a dead man in an alley, and instead of fleeing,

I had felt compelled to hold him tightly to me and absorb his energy into my body. I was already a predator who could consume human souls. My guilt swam around in my chest some days so much that it choked me. At other times, I could put it aside for a while. Today was going to be a choking sort of day, I figured.

I hadn't murdered the man, a nice guy named Marco Kendall. But I had absorbed him and later, used the energy I'd gotten from him to fight some bad guys who wanted to kill Castro.

Marco Kendall no longer existed. Not just because he was dead, but because I had consumed him and used him up. I had no idea how I could get the stain of that out of my soul.

Brooklyn came downstairs and handed her paper to Lucy, who had already scanned my minimal notes. She nodded. "Okay, looks like we got a winner. What I want is in the master suite. You all stay here. I need to do this next bit alone."

She put down her wineglass and went upstairs, leaving the four of us standing around the kitchen with nothing to do.

"Monitor," said Andre. "We can see what she's doing on there."

I didn't think Lucy would be stupid enough to leave the camera on once she got into the room, but who knows, maybe she'd forget about it. I followed the others into the dining room.

All of the monitors were off.

12

"You didn't take anything down, did you?" Castro asked while looking at Andre.

"Nope," said Andre. He checked to see that everything was plugged in and turned on. "It should be working."

"Maybe the batteries have run down," said Brooklyn. "When were they last switched out?"

Castro and Andre looked at each other. "I changed them around midnight, I think?" Castro said, though he sounded unsure.

"You're not sure you changed them, or you're not sure you did it at midnight?" I asked.

"I'm not sure of the time. I'm sure I switched them. The old ones should be recharged by now." He went to the battery chargers and pulled the batteries out. He stuck them in his pocket.

He headed toward the stairs, but a sudden thump from above stopped him. "What the hell?"

"What's she doing up there?" asked Andre at the same time.

"Let's find out," I said.

Brooklyn didn't look like she wanted to go up; I pointed at the dining room. "You can stay and watch the monitors." She nodded gratefully.

Castro took the steps two at a time. Andre and I followed slightly more slowly. I wasn't sure what the guys would see when they got to the master suite but it was Lucy's business to explain, not mine.

"She's not here," said Castro. Andre and I were in the room just after him. Castro glanced in the bathroom and shrugged. "Where did she go?"

I thought about the crawlspace above us. I pointed in that direction. "I think she's gone into the attic. From the closet."

Andre went to the camera. "Camera's turned off." He flicked a switch and called down the steps. "Can you see the bedroom now?"

"No," came the answer.

Andre switched out the batteries while Castro went to the closet and opened the door. If Lucy were upstairs, she had somehow pulled up the ladder and the trap door behind her.

"Up there?" he asked.

"Yep. We looked up in there yesterday afternoon. There's just some junk and exposed trusses."

"Bet there's tons of spiders," said Andre. "Attics are full of them."

"Thanks for that visual," said Castro. He reached up and pulled the trap door down. "Lucy?"

No response.

"Batteries changed," said Andre. He called down the stairs again. "Getting a picture?"

"Just static now."

"Damn it. Do you think she broke the camera?"

I shrugged. I had no idea what Lucy was willing to do in order to complete this chore for Ware. I doubted breaking a camera or two would weigh heavily on her conscience, assuming she even had one.

Castro pulled down the ladder. "I'm going to take a peek."

"Lucy?" I called up through the open hatch. "Castro's coming up."

"Stay away," she said. "This is the dangerous part."

Castro looked at me quizzically. I just shook my head. "I've never done this before. How should I know what's dangerous and what's not? Probably the best thing is to assume everything's dangerous."

"Where's the shadow? Did she take it up there with her?" asked Andre.

"Probably," I said, though I couldn't recall if Lucy had carried that lumpy sack with her up the stairs. Why couldn't I recall that? Sure, I was tired, but you'd think I'd want to keep track of a bag that had some kind of shadow person in it.

One that was prey for the scrap.

Oh. Sometimes, I'm slow. We had to catch the shadow so Lucy had the right bait. She wasn't going to do some kind of high-minded catch-and-release as she had said. She was simply going to feed the shadow to the scrap so she could get close enough to the papery thing to grab it.

My heart sank, even though I don't know why I was surprised. To these immortal creatures, humans were toys at best. Nuisances at worst. Our souls were clearly tools that they could use to accomplish their goals. The coldness of it hit me and I took a step back.

"What's up?" asked Andre.

My eyes teared up. "Nothing. Just realizing how, um, sad it is that these people's souls are trapped here, and we don't even know anything about them. Their names, when they died—nothing."

"At least Lucy's taking that one from the basement someplace safe."

When I didn't respond right away, Andre asked, "Well, isn't she?"

I wasn't sure how much I should say. Ware and Lucy wouldn't want Andre poking around in their business, but on the other hand, they didn't care about our souls, so why should we care about whatever their ultimate goals were?

"I doubt it," I said.

"Oh," said Andre. He glanced toward the attic space nervously. "Then why are we helping her?"

Good question. I just shot him a helpless look. As far as I knew, Ware had never lied to me. He'd refrained to saying anything, and he certainly didn't like to explain himself, but I don't think he'd ever lied. As amoral as he might be, he did seem to feel some kind of obligation to those he considered under his protection. And that meant me.

Lucy was something else. She had no obligation to me whatsoever. She was just a drinking buddy of Ware's. Beyond that, I didn't know anything about her feelings, or her desires, or her plans.

Castro has remained on the bottom step of the ladder and was looking back at Andre. He raised his eyebrows and shrugged. It was up to me to decide what I would tell Andre.

"My boss chose her to do this," I said, "and I had agreed to do this for my boss. I can't say why it's important to him, because he didn't say."

"He paying you for this?"

I nodded. "Basically, he's paying me for the shifts I'm missing at the bar. I don't know if he's paying Lucy or if she volunteered, or if this is something they do together all the time."

"You don't know much, do you?" asked Andre. He seemed a bit put out. "Your boss tells you to go ghost hunting and you just do it?"

"Hey," said Castro. "Ware's an odd duck, but if he wants to pay her to hang around a haunted house for a weekend, why not?"

"But is that payment enough?" asked Andre. He pointed up. "Why don't we just head back downstairs and let this creepy lady do whatever she plans to do? She says it's dangerous; I'm willing to believe her."

After watching the writhing, screaming shadow be forced into a bag by Lucy, I felt the same. Of course, I'd seen more crazy shit than Andre, but just that one thing would be enough for anyone, I'd think.

"Go on back downstairs," I said. "We'll stay up here in case she needs help."

Andre looked skeptical, but he left.

Castro headed up the ladder. "You need some help?" he called out.

"Didn't I say to stay away?" Lucy snapped back. "This part's dangerous."

"What isn't?" I muttered.

Castro stayed on the ladder and looked down at me. "Do I come down? Go up? What?"

I hesitated but finally said, "Come on down. If Ware sent her to do this, then we shouldn't need to interfere. Let her do whatever it is she's doing for him."

He came down the ladder and put an arm around my shoulder. "Shouldn't we know more? It seems that every time we turn around, we're in danger and we don't know enough to protect ourselves."

"Ware..."

"Ware doesn't necessarily have *my* best interests at heart, even if we assume he has yours," said Castro with a bit of heat. "And that's an assumption. As far as I'm concerned, he might feel some affection for you now, but the moment you cross him or become more liability than a help, he'll cut you loose. Then where will we be? In the middle of some kind of feud between immortal creatures with no way of defending or protecting ourselves. And it will all be Ware's fault."

I looked at him, surprised. He had never seemed to dislike my boss before. I couldn't dispute anything he said, though. Ware hadn't trusted me with a lot of information, and even that, he'd given grudgingly.

"Damn it," shouted Lucy.

Castro and I looked up to the dark hole that was the access to the attic. Four long black claws now curved around the edge. Slowly, four more claws appeared. Whatever was in the attic, it seemed prepared to leap down on us.

13

"Watch out down there," said Lucy. "Stay out of its way."

A face looked over the edge. Its eyes were flat black, but it was the bat-ears and the mouth full of sharp, pointed teeth that grabbed my attention. The scrap I'd seen in Ware's office had remained in the shadows; I'd heard it more than seen it. Now I was face-to-face with the thing I could become myself once I died. A scrap. A dead person with, if I believed Lucy, a divine ancestry.

The thing was the color of butcher paper, and, with its pointed ears and teeth and mushed-in nose, looked like the vampire bat I'd seen on a documentary a while back. Slightly lighter in color, but otherwise, almost a dead ringer. At least in the face. As it put its papery hands on the first rung of the ladder, its body came more into view.

It looked like a hairless monkey with a bat face. The incongruity of it, the sheer ridiculousness of what I was staring at, should have been funny. It was funny. In a dark way.

But the look on the thing's face was anything but amusing. Its face reflected nothing but rage and a desire to lash out at anything in its way.

Its gaze swept across Castro, dismissing him. Then it saw me and it froze. We stared at each other, the scrap and I.

Dizziness washed over me. This was someone like me, the soul of a person who had never asked to be different, probably never even knew they *were* different. Not until they died.

Since their death, they'd been this...this *thing*. I didn't know who this person had been in life, but they hadn't deserved this. An eternity as a little toothy monster? Spending forever in a rage, lashing out at the unfairness of it all, with no understanding of who you were, or what had happened, or why you were in such a state? Not knowing if it would ever end?

Tears dripped down my cheeks as I stared at it. "I'm sorry," I said under my breath.

The scrap opened its mouth and screamed. The sound was worse than fingernails on a chalkboard; my entire body shuddered at the way the sound pierced shot through my eardrums and pierced my skull. It resonated in every bone and sliced through every internal organ. It was the sound of pure despair.

The thing gathered itself, ready to leap. Without thinking, I shoved Castro aside and raised my right hand, showing the thing the brand on my palm.

It pulled up short and hissed.

Now I saw Lucy coming up behind it. "Good move," she said. Quickly, she knelt and grabbed the thing around its ribcage.

The scrap squealed and struggled, but Lucy had a firm grip on it. "Go on," she said through gritted teeth. "I've got it."

I kept my hand out. "Doesn't look like it to me," I said. A weird sensation began in my palm; a burning, then a tingling. It wasn't overtly painful, but it wasn't comfortable. I wanted nothing more than to retract my hand and do what Lucy said. I wanted no part of this.

Would it be me someday, wailing and struggling while Lucy wrapped her hands around *my* ribcage? Would I be shoved in a bag and be completely at the mercy of Lucy and Ware?

More tears ran down my face as the thing in Lucy's grip redoubled its efforts to free itself. "What are you going to do with it?" I asked.

Lucy had concentration only for the scrap. She didn't even glance my way as I said again, even louder, "What are you going to do with it?"

Castro pulled at my leg. "Maybe we should go."

Lucy pulled the thing back into the attic and disappeared into the darkness. Only the thumping and scraping of her struggle with it came from above now.

"We should go," said Castro. "Come on, Teryl."

I dropped my hand, but the tingling had moved up my arm. I shook my arm, wondering how long it would take the tingling to die down.

"Trouble?" asked Castro. "Does it hurt?"

"No, not really," I said. "Pins and needles mostly."

"You should have Ware explain that more carefully," he muttered. "If it's protection, you should know how to use it. If it's dangerous, you should know why and to whom it poses the greatest danger. It could be you, you know."

"Yeah," I said. "You know Ware won't say."

Castro shrugged. "Then quiz Fish. Offer him a free bottle of his favorite bourbon, and he'll probably open up."

A yelp came from the attic. "Damn thing," said Lucy.

This time, I went up the ladder.

Lucy sat in the chair we had seen in the attic earlier. She had her hands out in front of her, cupped, as if holding onto something large and invisible. In between her hands hovered the scrap.

At Lucy's feet was the lumpy sack containing the shadow person. The sack twisted and bumped in between Lucy's feet as if the thing inside were desperately trying to get out, but somehow, despite the fact the sack looked fairly flimsy and was only tied shut by a simple knot, the thing was failing to make any progress. Was it really that helpless, or did the sack have some kind of special power? Hell if I knew.

Lucy's face was a picture of concentration and frustration. The papery thing floated in between her hands and snapped its teeth at her face.

"Get out," Lucy managed to say while not breaking her concentration.

Behind her, something moved. A papery thing that looked like a cross between a bat head and a tailless, hairless monkey body slinked out from between two floor joists and bared its teeth at me.

Good freaking God, there were two of them. Before I could shout a warning to Lucy, the thing leaped at me.

14

On instinct, I held out my right hand and grabbed the lunging thing by the throat.

I almost let go; the moment the thing's papery skin met the brand on my palm, pain shot up my arm and seared its way through my muscles and bones. Tears sprung up in my eyes.

Honestly, how I kept my grip on the scrap was a mystery. But I did it.

I must have screamed or howled without knowing because Castro called up, "Teryl? You okay?"

I didn't have time to respond. The wriggling thing in my grip couldn't have weighed more than a few ounces, but it was strong. So strong.

But the pain from the mark on my hand faded and something else took over. A warmth seeped into my bones as I stared the thing eye to eye. Its flat black eyes didn't have pupils as far as I could tell in the dim light of the attic, but I had no doubt it was staring directly at me.

I felt slightly dizzy while I stared at it. It wrapped its clawed hands around my wrist and did its best to snap its jaws at me. But I kept my grip.

As the thing and I stared at each other, a strength welled up within my chest. It spread through my chest and down my arms and even flowed up my neck to wrap around my brain like some kind of internal hug. I leaned on that strength to return the stare of the thing.

Some kind of communication passed between us. Its anger and confusion pressed on my mind, threatening to send my thoughts into panic and chaos. Somehow, I felt its death; the final sharp pain in its chest, the inability to breathe, falling to the floor as the world faded to black.

And then, everything was different. Bigger, more colorful. The difference between day and night was no longer important. Emotions had narrowed to include rage and hatred but little else. I didn't understand the world around me anymore.

Pity flooded my thoughts. Was this how it had to be for people like me? The Lost? We died and became hateful little creatures that wanted nothing more than to take our rage out on the world around us? To consume the souls of others and be miserable?

No. There was something more. Just a glimmer, but a bit more. The thing looking at me saw something in me just as I saw something in it. Its soul reached into mine and felt some kind of kinship. I pitied it, and it...felt something toward me. Not pity. Not hate. Neither was it something warm and fuzzy like love or admiration. I wasn't sure what it was, because after a split second, before I could identify it, it was gone.

"Teryl?"

I blinked and the attic swam back into focus. My right hand was empty. Castro stood beside me with a hand on my shoulder.

Lucy, her bag, and the thing she'd been holding in midair between her outstretched hands were also gone.

"What?" I asked. "How long...?" I felt like I'd been kneeling on this floor for hours. My back ached and my head felt heavy. My right shoulder was sore as if I'd been holding up my arm without support for ages.

"How long since you came up here?" he asked. "Maybe fifteen seconds, maybe not that long. You screamed and I got up here as quickly as I could."

"Lucy?"

He shrugged. "Not up here."

No doubt she had caught the thing and taken it to Ware. What had happened to the second one was a mystery. I glanced around. "Did you see it?"

"See what, the weird munchkin thing?"

"A scrap," I said. "That's what Lucy called them."

"Them?"

"There were two. She had one. The other came at me and I grabbed it by the neck."

"So it's, like, dead?"

I shook my head. "I don't know what it is, but it's certainly not *dead*. Well, okay, it's a manifestation of a human soul, what's left over when someone like me dies. So, yeah, it's dead. But *I* didn't kill it. It was already that way."

Castro took a deep breath; his life was getting as weird as mine, what with papery human souls attacking people, shadow people that could be captured in bags, fallen angels everywhere, and a girlfriend with a magical rune on her hand. But, true to his weirdness-seeking nature, he took it with more grace than most, including me. He simply asked, "Now what?"

The attic felt lighter, airier that it had been before. "Whatever was here is gone," I said. "No reason to stay any longer, unless you feel like hanging out and eat more frozen pizza."

Castro ran a hand through his short black hair. "No, no need to stay. I'd like to get back to my own place, see Petunia, take a nap. Andre and I should start looking through the recordings, too, to see if we can document anything."

"Okay," I said. "Let's get back downstairs and tell the others we're packing up."

"Hey, you okay?" called Andre from the bottom of the ladder. "We thought we heard something like a scream. But it was kind of muffled, so we weren't sure."

"Everything's fine," I said.

"Did Lucy get the thing she was after?"

I looked at Castro, who gave me a sad smile and shrugged.

"I guess," I said. "She's gone, and so is it, and so is the bag."

Andre paused a moment. "I didn't see her leave."

"Neither did I," said Castro. "Maybe there's another entrance to this attic."

"Okay," said Andre doubtfully. "Weird, but okay, I guess."

"Since it seems Lucy has successfully cleared the house, let's pack up," said Castro. "There's nothing else to find here."

I sighed. "I guess I'll go to the bar and see if Ware's happy with the results of this little adventure."

"What does he want with these things, anyway?"

I shrugged. "Don't know. Not sure I want to, but I'll see what I can find out. Ignorance is not bliss in this case, I think."

Castro nodded, then did a double-take. "Oh."

"What?" I asked.

"There's something else that's gone." He pointed to where Lucy had been. "That chair."

I turned to look, and sure enough, the chair that had been in the attic had also disappeared.

Was it weird that this disturbed me? Maybe because it seemed so...unimportant? So mundane? A chair goes missing. Who cares, right?

I was pretty sure I needed to care, but I didn't know why I thought that. Add it to the list of things I needed to know, and that Ware was sure to not want to reveal.

15

Packing up took hardly any time at all. I dropped Castro, Andre, Brooklyn, and the equipment off at the building where Castro and I lived, and headed toward the bar. It was just after noon, and the Angels' Share wouldn't be open for a few hours yet, but Ware would be there, and possibly Fish as well.

I wondered if Lucy would also be there, or if she had merely dropped off her captured souls and had walked out of the bar and back into her ordinary life, whatever that was.

I parked down the street from the bar and got out of the car, allowing the bright blue of the autumn sky and the slight crispness of the air lighten my mood. Summer had been brutal, which was normal for St. Louis, but autumn was promising to be not only relief from the heat, but its bright colorful self. Spring in St. Louis can be a dreary mess of gloomy rainy days lasting for weeks at a time, but autumn was nearly always vibrant and beautiful.

The few trees the city had planted along the street sported some yellow leaves, and a few even fell at my feet as I walked down the street. Yes, autumn was definitely settling in.

I opened the door and walked into the dark interior of the Angels' Share. The bar was not the sort of place one came to watch sports and drink beer, or to sip wine while you sample the latest trendy arugula salad. This was the sort of place that sported ancient wood booths stained a deep chocolate, bartenders that remembered your favorite Scotch, and enough hard liquor to put down an army of elephants.

If you wanted food, cheer, or sports, you needed to go down the street to the *McGregor's Pub & Bar*. Yes, I know *pub* and *bar* are, more or less, synonyms, but nobody had apparently told McGregor that. Didn't seem to affect the quantity of sports fans who showed up there almost every night.

The Angels' Share was a place to drown sorrows, not cheer on the local sports team with one's buddies. With the Blues, the local hockey team, bringing home their first Stanley Cup ever recently, the city had gone crazy for sports even more than usual. Normally, the city was gaga for its first love, the baseball Cardinals.

I found it odd that the football Cardinals had left town over thirty years ago, but locals continued the tradition of saying *baseball Cardinals* as if there were still a need to differentiate between the two teams. Local customs are just weird, I guess.

Not as weird as the conversation I needed to have with my boss, though.

Fish was indeed present, drinking a bottle of something honey-colored in a back booth. I suppose he was taking Ware up on the free alcohol offer and would be occupying the booth for the rest of the day. Good thing these supernatural creatures either didn't have livers, or had livers that merely laughed at large quantities of alcohol.

I started to wave at Fish, but he was staring intently into his half-full glass, so I just went to Ware's office door and knocked under the "Private" sign he had posted on it.

A few moments later, the door opened a couple of inches. "Ah, Teryl," said Ware. "I didn't expect you until tomorrow."

He opened the door and stepped out, which I expected. I had only ever been allowed into his office once, and I wasn't eager to go in again, knowing he had a scrap back there. That one had brushed against my ankles and even thinking about the way it had slithered past my feet still made me shudder.

Ware wasn't overly tall, just a bit taller than me, but shorter than Fish or Castro. He was barrel-chested, white-haired, and had white eyebrows tipped in black. The sense of authority and power that emanated from him was almost electric; when he stood next to Lucy or Fish or another of his own kind, the sense was even stronger. Among the Forlorn, he was a formidable power, and an authority to be reckoned with. Yet he spent his time in his office and rarely came out; instead, he sent others, like Lucy, to do his bidding.

"Lucy took care of everything this morning," I said. "I figured she'd have come back here by now to deliver whatever it was you wanted."

"Whatever it was?" Ware asked with some humor. "You must have seen it."

"A scrap, yes," I said, before correcting myself. "Scraps. And there was a shadow person she caught in a bag. I don't know what combination of those things you were looking for, but she had them at least an hour ago, and she just disappeared. The rest of us packed up our equipment, and I dropped everyone else off, or I could have been here earlier. She should have beaten me here. Or is she taking those things somewhere else for you?"

Ware's face showed concern. "Wait. You said *scraps?* There was more than one?"

That made Fish look up.

"There were two. They both seem to be gone so I assume Lucy got them all." I didn't mention I felt she was going to feed the shadow person to the scraps. If I didn't say it, would it be something I could continue to deny, even though my suspicion that it was true was very strong?

Ware crossed his arms and closed his eyes. "Two scraps? Huh. I sent her to reconnoiter the place last week, and she didn't say anything about that."

"Maybe she only saw one."

Ware opened his eyes to glare at me. "Someone like Lucy, who's been hunting scraps for centuries, knows how to sense them and count them before engaging in the hunt. She mentioned one, not two."

"Oh." I didn't know what else to say.

"What else?" asked Fish, injecting himself into the conversation.

"What do you mean?" asked Ware.

"What else did she take?"

Ware froze. I didn't understand the implications of Fish's question, but Ware obviously did. His gaze swung from Fish to me and now he was deadly serious. "Did she take anything else?" he asked in a low voice that was almost a growl.

I backed up, startled by the intensity of the glare, heart pounding. Had I done something wrong? Would Ware be upset with me? The thought chilled me to the very marrow.

"Ah, um, a chair? Maybe a kid's music box, but the chair, definitely."

"Bitch," said Ware sharply. He broke off the glare and shook his head as if to clear it. "Thought I could trust her."

Fish grabbed his bottle, as if afraid Ware would now take it from him.

I wanted to ask what was so important about a chair, but at the same time, I wanted to be invisible so Ware wouldn't stare at me again. I wanted to go home and hide under my covers while the Forlorn argued and fought somewhere else.

I wanted to be safe from these creatures. I didn't see that as an option, though. Not really. Not, apparently, ever, if Lucy's little story about Gilgamesh were actually real and not just something she'd made up to freak me out.

Ware took in a deep breath and visibly tried to calm himself. "Where would she go?" he asked no one in particular. He must know I wouldn't have any clue, and Fish didn't seem like the kind to keep track of Ware's drinking buddies.

"What is she going to do?" I managed to squeak out.

Ware hesitated, then said, "You remember I told you a little about *sinkholes*? About the kinds of places we Forlorn could use to escape this world?"

I nodded. After thousands, if not tens of thousands, of years here, life on earth for some of the Forlorn apparently got to be too much to take. They wanted to go to pocket universes of their own creation and, well, *retire* there. I wasn't entirely clear on that that meant, but that's what Ware had told me.

"She wants to make a sinkhole of her own?" I asked.

"Yes," said Ware with a grimace.

"No," said Fish. He said it softly, but the word hung in the air like the peal of a bell.

Once again, Ware swung to face Fish. He didn't ask the obvious question, but he clearly wanted to. Every muscle fiber in his body appeared to be trembling. He feared the answer, feared it too much to say the question out loud. But he still needed to know. I grabbed onto the edge of the bar and hung on to keep my balance. The air around me seemed to shift, become heavy, become toxic somehow. I had no idea how Ware did that, or if he were even aware of it. Maybe the atmosphere of this place reflected his moods whether he wanted it to or not.

"She wants to get to *him*. You know she does," said Fish. "She doesn't want to spend the rest of eternity in a backwater universe all by herself. She wants to be his queen. She wants to rule."

Rule?

"Rule what?" I asked.

Ware wavered on his feet and put a hand to the doorjamb to steady himself. I'd never seen him in this state before. He was terrified.

Fish's eyes were downcast, but the set of his shoulders was tight, as if he were also frightened. His fingers clenched the bottle in front of him so tightly they were white and bloodless.

"Rule what?" I asked again, alarm rising in my voice.

Fish looked up at me sadly. "The universe."

16

I laughed out loud, despite the shocked look of terror on Ware's face. "Rule the universe? Are you nuts? You understand that makes Lucy sound like some cartoon villain."

Fish seemed to collapse in on himself. "If *he* were to come back, the war would start up just like last time. And this time, there'd be no holding back. She's fought beside him before. She'd do it again." He looked at Ware sadly. "I didn't disagree when you forgave her last time. He was gone and it seemed safe enough to let a few of his confederates roam free as long as they promised to behave. Then she joined your little club, and I thought maybe she'd changed. But I guess not. She was never on your side."

"Wait, do you mean that crazy story about a war was true?" I asked.

"What story?" asked Ware.

I gave a helpless shrug. "Last night, Lucy fed me and Brooklyn some story about a war and the two leaders who both loved the same woman, and about how this woman had a child with some human guy. I thought she was jerking my chain, and of course, Brooklyn thought it was just a myth."

"Brooklyn?"

"Andre's cousin." Before he could ask about Andre, I said, "Andre is Castro's friend. He goes ghost hunting fairly regularly, I think. Brooklyn's supposedly psychic or sensitive to ghosts or something, and she was currently living with Andre, so he brought her along."

Ware stared at me briefly, then shook his head. "I didn't think you'd involve others in this."

"Castro did," I said, though I realized that sounded like I was making excuses. "But you didn't say not to, and I had no idea what to expect, so I figured it was fine. When they showed, I thought they could help spell us so we could sleep in shifts. In the end, though, Lucy pretty much took care of everything."

Ware closed his eyes, still looking as if he might collapse in shock or terror. "And now she has two scraps, and the chair. No wonder she was so eager to go to that house. She'd probably tracked it down months ago."

"What's so special about this chair?"

Ware looked at me; his black eyes boring into mine. "Was it a simple chair without paint or adornment? It wouldn't have looked special at all."

"It looked absolutely ordinary. There have to be thousands like it."

"Yes and no. It was made by the Shakers, so it was hardly unique in its construction. But this one had something special. If you'd examined it closely, you would have found a few small brown stains on it."

"Blood," I said baldly, because what else would these creatures get so worked up about? Not barbecue sauce.

"Yes."

"Whose blood?"

Ware finally let go of the doorjamb. "Mine. I was trying to...to make something that would help me create and control more sinkholes. The chair...I thought I'd lost it."

"Lost," I said. I didn't dare say more out loud, but why would a powerful creature like Ware try to make some kind of magical object and then just *lose* it.

"There was a fire downtown," he said. "In 1849. The steamboat *White Cloud* exploded and a lot of the city burned to the ground. That year was a bad one for St. Louis, because of the fire and also the cholera outbreak. At least ten per cent of the city's citizens perished. In the chaos of that year, it appeared to me the chair had been destroyed, either in the fire, or later by those it made homeless, as they pillaged every garbage dump for wood to burn for heat or cook their food. I hunted for the chair, but never had any real hope of finding it. It seems Lucy was finally able to track it down."

I wanted to say *maybe you should have looked harder,* but I didn't. I doubted it was easy to make one of the Forlorn bleed, and a chair infused with angel blood had to be special enough that it wouldn't just burn up in an ordinary fire.

Or maybe it would. It wasn't like Ware was good about telling me all of the rules about what being Forlorn actually meant.

"Now she has the means to make a sinkhole?" I glanced at Fish and remembered what he'd said. "Or, find another sinkhole that's already been discovered. Where *he* is, whoever this *he* person is."

Ware nodded.

"And that's bad."

He nodded again.

My heart sank into my gut. "I guess that means someone has to find her, and get the chair back? Or get the scraps away from her?"

Or both? But I didn't want to say that. I had no idea how to find Lucy, let alone how to get something she wanted badly away from her. Let Ware handle this.

"You know who would know where she is," said Fish. "I don't have his number."

Ware hesitated and looked at me evenly. "Maybe there's another way. Yama..."

Yama was one of Ware's drinking buddies, much like Lucy. Each one of these creatures had certain talents that was either theirs alone, or were shared by very few. Yama had the special skill of being able to track down his fellow Forlorn.

"Is out of town," said Fish.

"There's no one else who can track other Forlorn besides Yama?" I asked.

"Mink," said Fish. "You have a number for her?"

Ware shook his head. "Haven't seen her in forty years, at least. She might be around, but she's not that fond of this area. She prefers the Far East. You know that."

"I wouldn't expect her to keep in contact with me, but she might touch base with you every now and again. How am I to know? But if not Mink, then there's only him left, if you need someone local."

Another *he* that no one seemed interested in naming. "So, if you actually name this guy, will he hear you, like You-Know-Who in Harry Potter?"

"Like who?" asked Ware, baffled. Guess the Harry Potter books hadn't been on his reading list.

"Evil wizard in a book," said Fish. "No, he can't hear his name being spoken aloud at a distance. It's just that he's not somebody you like."

I knew less than a dozen of these fallen angels and there were several I didn't like. So that hardly narrowed it down.

I waited.

Ware sighed. "Pellagrio. He can be a bully."

"No shit," I said. I'd only seen the guy a couple of times, and neither encounter had left me with a positive feeling toward him.

On the other hand, I can handle jerks. You can't be a bartender for long and be helpless before idiots who think they're the first one to tell you you're pretty or to grab your butt or who look for some excuse to follow you to your car.

I recalled the tall man's stern face, the way his hair was almost striped between dark auburn and dirty white. He had an air of solidity about him, as if, should be decide to be immovable, he would be truly planted in place, unwavering and absolutely still. The world might crumble around him, and he would be in the same place, and would stay there until he willed himself to move.

"And he'll know where to find Lucy?"

"Probably," said Ware. "I'll call him." He disappeared back into his office.

Once Ware had gone, I walked over to Fish. "So, why is Pellagrio the one who will know where Lucy is?"

He lifted tired dark brown eyes to meet mine. "They've been close since forever. Kind of like brother and sister, although our kind don't have siblings. But they've always just...hung out, shared their thoughts. You know, like BFFs."

"So why is she Ware's drinking buddy, and he isn't? It seems she isn't such a fan of Ware, and Pellagrio certainly isn't."

"She likes Oya, for one thing," said Fish. "And she and Truck used to be lovers. So, when she started showing up with Oya and Truck, I think Ware just let her stay. Maybe she wanted to keep an eye on him, too."

"Because she's a fan of this other guy. Does he have a name?"

"Of course," said Fish. "But I don't think I'll be the one to tell you about him. That's for Ware to do."

"Since Ware and this other dude had a war, and they both loved the same woman, and then everything went to the crapper when she died, and, what, the war was just interrupted and is ready to start up again? Like, Lucy will bring this other guy back around and, poof, everyone's picking sides and fighting again?"

Fish took a pull from the bottle. It was Old Crow, one of the cheapest things we had on the shelf. The sort of stuff that would, as they say, put hair on your chest. It was harsh stuff; clearly, Ware wanted to give Fish some kind of reward but nothing too fancy.

Finally, Fish put the bottle back down. "Something like that."

"Which side were you on?" I asked, suddenly curious.

"I did my best not to pick one," he said. "Why do you think I'm never in the cool kids club like Oya and Yama?"

"Oh." I wasn't sure if this made me feel better about Fish or not. On the one hand, trying to stay neutral when everyone around you was trying to kill each other was probably what I'd try to do. On the other, you have to wonder about somebody who has no loyalties except to himself.

Of course, that was for humans. With the Forlorn, how could I judge? I was neither an immortal being, nor something that had spent the first part of my existence flying around the universe doing...I don't know, whatever powerful solitary winged immortal creatures do. My imagination failed me there. If I couldn't even wrap my head around the kind of life they'd lead, how could I know or judge anything about them?

"Pellagrio was on the other side?"

"Yep."

"But Ware let him go, too."

"Eh, not so much let him go as didn't pursue him terribly hard. Pellagrio, at least, isn't a duplicitous, backstabbing son of a bitch like Marveaux," he said, mentioning one of the Forlorn that had tried to kill Castro a few weeks ago. "Pellagrio's an ass, but you can trust him to keep his word. He's solid like that. When he said he wouldn't keep the war going, that he would live and let live, Ware believed him. And, as far as I know, he's done that."

"So if he says he'll help me find Lucy, he will."

"Sure," said Fish. He finished off the bottle and put it down on the table. "But if I were you, I'd pay more attention to what he *doesn't* say."

That did not reassure me in the slightest.

17

An hour later, I stood in front of a Victorian house near Lafayette Square. It wasn't, in fact, that far from where Oya lived. I guess Lucy liked to keep close to her friend for some reason, or at the very least, they appreciated the same style of house.

The day had turned gloomy, the way autumn days sometimes did. Clouds had skittered across the sky as if they were late for some appointment further east. Darker, thicker clouds had followed on that first set's heels and had parked themselves over the city. The air now had a chill in it that it hadn't before, and it smelled of fallen leaves and dampness.

If yesterday's sun had been a tribute to the summer that had just passed, today was a nod toward the spooky and dark season of Halloween and the end of daylight saving time. In fact, Lucy's neighbors already had a scarecrow and a skeleton in their front yard. I shivered at the chill and thought briefly about my own Halloween decorations, currently sitting in my apartment's storage space in the building's basement. Since meeting actual monsters in real life, the appeal of putting out fake decorative ones had diminished significantly. What was the fun of putting up a cartoon ghost when I now knew that I'd be turning into a butcher-paper brown, toothy bat-monkey thing when I died? And that I might very well end up being hunted by one of the Forlorn and then used, or even destroyed, for their own purposes?

It wasn't much to look forward to, and it made me envy the silly sheet-covered spirits that floated around going "boo."

The wind had picked up some of the fallen leaves in the street and swirled them around my feet. Beside me, Pellagrio stood solid and tall as he stared at the house. "She's home," he said.

"Just like that?" It seemed odd Lucy would betray Ware and then simply *go home*. Maybe she figured that would be the last place he would look, or maybe she thought that, since he didn't know where she lived, it was safe. She probably hadn't counted on Ware contacting Pellagrio.

"Just like that," he said. "Let me go first."

I nodded, though he had already started forward. I didn't know why he wanted to be in front, but that was fine with me.

The wind picked up his bi-colored air and blew it around his head in an odd aureole. He didn't appear to notice; but then, he seemed like the sort of person who never noticed personal comfort or the weather.

He hadn't said ten words to me so far, and I was glad of that. Though now that he was, more or less, behaving and not being a world-class jerk to me, I was becoming more curious about him. Why had he signed up with the other side? What was it about Ware that he had not liked, or at least why had he liked the other guy better?

Had he, too, loved this mysterious female angel who'd captured Ware's heart? Who was she and what had she been like? If it were true she had produced a child with a human, why had she done that? What was it that *she* had planned?

I sighed. Too many questions, and I didn't have enough trust in any of the Forlorn around me to give me straight answers.

Pellagrio tried the door, which was locked. He reached into his pocket and extracted a key. So he and Lucy were close enough to exchange keys. Interesting.

It made me wary. Despite what Pellagrio had said about helping me get the chair and the scraps away from Lucy, Fish's warning about listening to what Pellagrio *didn't* say rang in my head. He hadn't specifically said he'd see me safely back to the bar, or that he'd protect me in a fight. He'd just said he'd help acquire the things Ware wanted.

It was clear that Ware wanted me safe as well, but neither he nor Pellagrio had specifically said that out loud or made it part of the deal. Maybe Pellagrio could be trusted to know that Ware would be pissed if I were harmed, and would seek to make sure I was safe. Ware should know if Pellagrio could be trusted with my safety.

Pellagrio opened the door and we went inside. The interior of the house was decorated much as Lucy decorated herself; it looked like it had been lost in a time warp since sometime in the 1960s. Wood paneling, wood furniture with the little legs—I'm pretty sure I'd heard my mother call it *mid-century modern* at some point—beaded curtains and everything in gold and olive green.

I guess there was something to be said for being attracted to a certain style and keeping with it over the decades. No one had ever accused me of having a style besides *garage sale kitsch*.

Something skittered behind me. I whirled around but saw only more mid-century modern furniture, this time a dining room set. Horrible florid wallpaper covered the far wall while mirrors covered one of the other walls.

Another scrap? How many of these things were there?

Pellagrio swung his head around as if listening. If he'd heard the scrap, he didn't give any indication. He simply nodded toward the far corner of the house and said, "Basement."

Great. I just nodded as Pellagrio headed through several large rooms full of wooden furniture and through a small room that contained only boxes. I would have thought it was a corridor but it didn't go anywhere.

"Old butler's pantry," said Pellagrio as I slowed down to look at the box-filled space. "Not important."

For the moment, I had to trust that he knew what was important and what wasn't. Sure as hell I didn't know.

The slight swishing sound of a creeping scrap came from behind me. I tensed but didn't turn around. Would the damn thing attack, or was it merely trying to bring up the rear so we'd be surrounded once we got downstairs?

Pellagrio continued to ignore it. Considering the keenness of Lucy and Ware's hearing, I doubted he hadn't heard it. If my mortal ears were capable, his immortal ones certainly were.

"We're being followed," I said.

"So what?"

Well, that was that. He knew, and he didn't care, and he had me between him and the scrap. Of course, he was between me and Lucy, so...which was better?

Pellagrio tromped down the stairs; I followed more slowly and carefully. The stairs were steep and wooden and had no handrail. I kept my hands on the walls to either side and did my best to keep my balance.

"Melusine," said Pellagrio. Or something like that. I recalled someone had told me Lucy was short for something, but I hadn't remembered what.

I got to the bottom of the steps and stood on the dirt floor of an old cellar. The floor joists of the house were just over my head; this space was cramped, damp, and uncomfortable to be in. A bit of light from outside shone in from the far wall, where the street was. An old coal chute?

Lucy sat in the chair in the middle of the room. She had drawn more symbols around her, this time in salt, or at least something white and powdery. I guess sidewalk chalk didn't work on dirt that well.

The bag she had captured the shadow person in was open and empty at her feet. On her lap sat one of the scraps. It trembled in either fear or rage; its weird bat-like face could have been reflecting either emotion as far as I could tell.

Lucy's eyes were closed; her hands were spread out over the scrap as if providing it with a blessing. Which was probably exactly the opposite of what she was trying to do.

Her face was red with concentration and she was biting her bottom lip. Dark hair hung in her face and down her arms to pool around the trapped scrap.

Pellagrio took in the sight carefully and crossed his arms, his feet slightly apart. He now had that immovable quality that seemed to permeate his whole being at times. Whatever it was he wanted, he wasn't leaving this spot until he got it.

"*Water Flowing in the Heart of the Stars*," he said softly.

Lucy's eyes blinked open at that. I had realized a few weeks ago that these creatures had had far different names before arriving on earth, names that apparently could be glossed, if not truly translated, into English. I had to assume this was Lucy's.

Lucy saw Pellagrio first and the ghost of a smile crossed her face, but then she noticed me hanging back at the base of the steps, and she sneered, the smile completely wiped out in an instant. "What's she doing here? Did you decide to run an errand for *Ware*?"

"More for myself," he said. "I wanted to know if you were truly trying to do something this stupid. I had hoped Ware was wrong, and I'd be able to fling that back in his face." Sadness dripped from his voice.

"Stupid? You fought beside me, under *his* command. Not Ware's. We've lived with him loose in the world long enough. It is time to make a change."

Pellagrio shook his head. "No, it isn't. Perhaps someday. But not today. Not any time in the near future. Our master only wanted destruction at the end. His high ideals died over the eons until there was nothing but anger and hatred left to him."

"Then that's what the universe should have of him," said Lucy. "He is our commander, our master. Ware is nothing beside him."

A grumble came from Pellagrio's chest. Was that a laugh? I couldn't tell. "Seems to me they were pretty equally matched," he said without anger or sadness. "And he's kept to himself, more or less, since then. He hasn't bothered me and he offered you friendship without bringing up your past, which you know some would have done."

"So, you're on his side now?"

"Side? What side? There are no sides. The war was stupid and ultimately pointless. Worlds that should hang in the sky are gone now. Species that never harmed us were crushed under our feet, extinct forever. Beauty that captivated all of us was ruined, smeared across the galaxies like so much shit. Zireya *died*. And for what? So Ware and our master could have some kind of universe-wrecking pissing contest? Fuck it, Lucy, what's the point of this all?"

"It's not fair!" she howled. "Ware is free. He should have died with Zireya. Or at least be trapped in his own damn sinkhole."

Pellagrio didn't move.

"And *her*," now Lucy pointed at me. "Walking around with Zireya's face. Not having any idea of who she is or what she might be capable of. Ware protecting her without telling her anything." She focused on me. "Tell me, human, do you trust him? You shouldn't. He'll keep you in the dark until you no longer prove useful to him, and then he'll end you."

That sounded like it just might be the truth, but I could hardly say I trusted Lucy or Pellagrio. Maybe Fish, but he was clearly a lesser member of this race, hardly strong enough to stand up to Lucy, let alone Ware. He wasn't someone to turn to for protection.

"What choice do I have?" I asked. "It's him or...you? Oya? Marveaux? None of you has my well-being at heart. I'm just a mortal who will be here for a few years and then I'll be dead. What do any of you care?"

"We don't," said Pellagrio in his solid voice.

"Thanks," I said.

"Sarcasm suits you," he said. "Now, Melusine, give this up. Destroy the scraps or turn them over to Ware as you agreed. Forget the war. Drink yourself into oblivion like everybody else, and wait for the ages to turn again. We'll get off this rock eventually."

"And get our wings back?" Lucy asked. "Do you remember my wings? How green they were! Every feather tipped in white." Tears ran down her face. "How can you live without yours? I can't live without mine!"

Another grumble from Pellagrio. "You already have. There's no need for all this drama. Do the right thing. Give this up. Get the scraps in the bag and let's go to the bar."

Lucy finally registered what he was saying. "Scraps? I only have the one."

"Then what's that one doing behind us?" I asked. I turned slowly. The other scrap sat on the stairs, teeth bared, black eyes focused directly on me.

112/Marella Sands

18

The scrap and I kept our eyes locked on each other. I saw the tension in its muscles and prayed it wouldn't leap for my face.

"That one's not mine," said Lucy. "I left it in the house, hoping it would chew up the humans, make them regret ever going there."

"Why?" I asked as I stared down the creature on the stairs.

"Because it would be fun to know those stupid ghost hunters had been mauled by what *really* haunts houses."

"Sounds amusing," said Pellagrio. "But do you really want to make an enemy of Ware?"

"He's always been my enemy."

"Always is a long time, as we both know," said Pellagrio. "There's nothing that lasts *always*, not even us."

"Close enough," Lucy hissed. "Now get out. I'm going to find him and I'm going to bring him back to this world and we will rule it. And from here, we will go wherever we wish, and bring blessing or destruction, depending on our mood. No one will stand against us."

"Ware will," said Pellagrio. While Lucy's voice had risen in pitch and had become strident, Pellagrio's voice sounded the same as ever. Solid, as if his opinion or his thoughts were clear and unchanging.

"We'll take care of him," said Lucy. She did something that made her grunt, but I didn't dare turn around while the scrap stared at me.

Whatever it was Lucy did, it distracted the scrap and it let out a mournful cry. A moment later, that was followed by a scream from behind me. I whirled around and saw Lucy crushing the scrap in her hands. Bones in its papery body crushed under her fingers, and black blood oozed out of a dozen wounds its broken bones pierced through its flesh and skin.

"No!" I yelled.

Something hit me in the shoulder and I jumped. I tried to brush the scrap off, but it clung to my shirt and hissed at Lucy.

Lucy paid no attention; she concentrated on dribbling the scrap's blood on herself, the floor around her, and the chair. Shadows began gathering around her and everything near her started to go out of focus. I blinked but couldn't truly get my eyes to settle on any one thing.

The thing in Lucy's hands made a desperate mewling sound and I leaped forward, hands out, as if to grab it. I had no idea why; the thing would have mauled me if it were free.

The scrap on my shoulder leaped forward at Lucy, clawed hands outstretched, but bounced off an invisible barrier. My hands also came across something unyielding in between me and Lucy. It coincided with the salt lines on the floor.

The scrap that had just been on my shoulder tried desperately to get to its companion, but kept being repelled. It hissed and squawked, clearly enraged, and willing to hurt itself in its fury and distress.

The scene inside the salt glyph got more bizarre. The shadows swirled around Lucy; they weren't shadows like the shadow person had been and they weren't normal shadows like what was cast by the sun. In fact, *shadow* wasn't a great word for them, but I didn't know what else to use. The things flitted along solid surfaces like the chair's legs but then leaped to the barrier and back again. They were three dimensional, then two dimensional...my mind refused to take it all in.

A line from a movie ran through my head; *this non-Euclidian geometry is shit.* I hadn't really gotten it then, but I got it now. What should have been right angles weren't, what should have been triangles had a multitude of sides I couldn't see except, somehow, out of the corner of my eyes. My head swam and my stomach threatened to rebel at the dizzying colors and angles.

Over everything was the form of Lucy, hands still wrapped around the scrap. Her face morphed into something long an angular, her shoulders widened as if to accommodate the wings she'd once had on her back. Her skin was like ivory; her eyes sparkled like emeralds and her hair swirled around her head like a dark crown.

I'd seen something similar a few weeks ago when Yama had shifted his form in a vision I'd been forced to witness inside my head while Oya possessed my body. These creatures didn't look human in their original form; they were angular, hard, and almost metallic, as if carved from primal elements rather than being formed of softer materials like mere flesh. Their faces had eyes and mouths but their teeth were many and pointed, their cheekbones wide and sharp as razor wire. Nothing about them was curved or fluid; they were all angles and planes.

A vision of wings appeared behind her, though they were insubstantial. I didn't think she could get her wings back; like Oya had done, Lucy was somehow bringing the *thought* of them back merely by the intensity of her longing for them. But they weren't real. They were a sea-foam green, with each feather shading toward white at the tip, at least from the shadowy forms of them that I could see. They were achingly beautiful, but I couldn't look at them for long; the emerald-green eyes in the sharp jutting ivory face were far too frightening to be ignored for long

I eased my foot forward and managed to scrape a tiny bit of salt away from the lines at my feet. Encouraged, I moved my foot a little more. The scrap on the floor watched me, then moved a clawed hand toward the salt and managed to push aside a few grains on its own.

I tried again. So did the scrap. Between the two of us, we managed to make some progress, but it was slow. Too slow.

The scrap looked at me and chirped. I had no idea what that meant, but somehow, a thought came to me. I held out my hand and the scrap stood as tall as it could and wrapped its bone-thin fingers around my middle finger. A cold power flowed from it into me. The scrap was giving me some of its soul. I could feel it.

Now I could move more salt aside. Then more. In a few moments, I had completely broken one of the salt lines.

Lucy's head pitched back and she screamed. The swirling shapes around her faded, as did her strange angular form and her dream wings. Only the Woodstock refugee sat before me now, a brown body on her lap, and her hands and clothes stained with black blood.

The scrap let go of my finger and leaped for her. She swatted it aside. I jumped at her and got my hands around her neck as she struggled to stand up from the chair.

The chair, however, seemed to have a hold of her. I could see no restraints, no chains, yet Lucy was unable to stand. She batted at me with her arms while the scrap jumped on her head and scratched at her eyes.

I pitched over, unbalanced, but didn't let go of Lucy. Both of us, and the chair, fell onto the floor.

"No, no, no, no, no!" she screamed. "I will find him! Get off me, you stupid bitch!"

"Stop," said Pellagrio.

Lucy almost immediately went limp.

I kept my hands around her neck but she didn't seem to notice, which infuriated me. I redoubled my efforts.

Pellagrio stood before me, offering me a hand up. "If you think we're that easy to kill, you haven't learned much about us yet. You can't hurt her with your hands."

I didn't want to listen, but I knew it was true; these creatures weren't subject to things like death from strangulation. Unwillingly, I removed my fingers, one by one, from around her neck. Lucy just lay limp on the floor, still stuck, somehow, to their chair.

"I'll take care of her," said Pellagrio.

"What does that mean?"

"Ware will want to put her somewhere he has control over. I'm not sure I'm going to agree to that. But clearly, she's gotten in over her head, or her ass wouldn't be stuck to that chair. I'll take her somewhere she can't be a danger to anyone while I figure this out."

"What if I say no," I said. "What if I said you should take her to Ware and let him do whatever he wants to her?"

"I think you should remember he's the one who got you into this mess in the first place. Do you really trust him?"

He was right, and he was wrong. Ware had sent me here tonight, but if Lucy's story were true, I was, by virtue of being descended from the one-and-only angel-human cross, going to be involved, whether I liked it or not. Ware didn't get me into this. My genes did.

The other scrap pawed its dead companion.

"What about this scrap?" I asked.

"That's up to you," said Pellagrio and he grabbed the chair and hauled it up, Lucy still hanging limply from it.

"What do you mean? Once it notices me again, it'll go right for my face."

Pellagrio shook his head. "I don't know what you did, but you've bound it to you. It's yours now, like the one in Ware's office is his."

My mind almost refused to take that in. I had a pet scrap? How had that even happened?

It made no sense.

I opened my mouth to protest, but Pellagrio and his burden were gone. The scrap at my feet chirped and hopped onto my shoulder.

I tried to get a good look at it, but it was too close to my face to focus on. "So...," I said. "You're with me now?"

The thing flicked black blood off of its claws. "Sorry about your friend," I said. It only shook its bat-head and scratched itself on the shoulder with a black-stained hand.

I took a last look around the basement. Salt was everywhere, but no longer appeared to be distributed in some kind of symbol-like fashion. Anyone who came down here now would just think someone had spilled a package of salt.

I sighed and climbed the steps. The scrap wrapped an arm around my neck to help it keep its balance on my shoulder.

Home called to me, but I didn't think showing up there with a scrap on my shoulder would be wise. I needed to go to the bar. I needed to talk with Ware.

The thought made me wearier than I had ever been. I stumbled out into the fading daylight and got behind the wheel of my car and cried.

The scrap hopped down and sat itself in the passenger seat. I could barely even look at it. I should be terrified of this thing, but I was already thinking of how I was going to live with it in my life. Would it attack Castro? Would it eat our pet hedgehog Petunia? Would it be visible to others? Would I have to hide it like Ware did the one in his office? Or would it be invisible most of the time? I had questions, but no answers. Ware should be able to answer them, if he could be convinced to. For now, I felt too weary to argue with him, but I'd have to ask him, anyway.

I longed to go home, shove my face in my pillow, and forget everything. *Home.* Castro, Petunia, my own things. But that had to come second.

Eventually, I managed to calm myself and I started the car. I put it on the road back to the Angels' Share and debated what I would ask my boss first.

Whatever it was, I didn't think he would like it. The thought weighed on me as the first stars came out as if everything were normal.

The scrap chirped as if excited about the car ride. I shuddered at the sound.

Normal? Not a word I got to use anymore.

About the Author

Marella Sands is a native St. Louisan who has published novels, short stories, and non-fiction works. Her historical novels, *Sky Knife* and *Serpent and Storm*, were set in 5th century Central America. *Sky Knife* has also appeared in a German edition as *Der Mayapriester*. In addition, she co-wrote two King's Quest novels with fellow St. Louisan Mark Sumner under the name Kenyon Morr. She has had short stories in several anthologies. She has always been interested in cemeteries, sits on the board of one, and also is a volunteer at Cahokia Mounds State Historic Site in Collinsville, Illinois (horseradish capital of the world and home of the world's largest ketchup bottle!). She and her husband travel whenever they can and stop by old cemeteries when they have the opportunity.

Marella earned degrees in anthropology from the University of Tulsa and Kent State University. The author's household includes the author, her husband, and a multitude of pets.

Word Posse Fun Fact

This book is perhaps the logical extension of my early reading habits. I read every John Keel and Erich von Däniken book I could find. My copy of D. Scott Rogo's *Haunted House Handbook* has been read so many times, it's falling apart. So naturally, I would want to put the paranormal in my books and have ghost hunter characters show up to play with the EMF meters and record EVPs. Full disclosure: even after a lifetime of reading about the topic and visiting allegedly haunted locations, I have not, so far, come across any particularly convincing evidence that the paranormal actually exists. But who knows what will happen tomorrow...

www.ingramcontent.com/pod-product-compliance
Lightning Source LLC
Chambersburg PA
CBHW060641130626
46555CB00002B/903

* 9 7 8 1 9 4 4 0 8 9 1 5 3 *